A CHRISTMAS SONG FOR THE PRESTWICH ORPHAN

CHRISTMAS VICTORIAN ROMANCE

DOLLY PRICE

PUREREAD.COM

Copyright © 2023 PureRead Ltd

www.pureread.com

All rights reserved. No part of this publication may be reproduced, distributed or transmitted in any form or by any means, without prior written permission.

Publisher's Note: This is a work of fiction. Names, characters, places, and incidents are a product of the author's imagination. Locales and public names are sometimes used for atmospheric purposes. Any resemblance to actual people, living or dead, or to businesses, companies, events, institutions, or locales is completely coincidental.

CONTENTS

Dear reader, get ready for another great story…	1
Chapter 1	3
Chapter 2	16
Chapter 3	33
Chapter 4	44
Chapter 5	60
Chapter 6	74
Chapter 7	90
Chapter 8	103
Chapter 9	117
Chapter 10	129
Chapter 11	141
Chapter 12	154
Chapter 13	170
Chapter 14	192
Chapter 15	207
Epilogue	220
Love Victorian Christmas Saga Romance?	231
Have You Read?	235
Our Gift To You	247

DEAR READER, GET READY FOR ANOTHER GREAT STORY...

❄

A CHRISTMAS VICTORIAN ROMANCE

On the cold Manchester streets, Georgina's life is a cycle of thievery and torment, until a chance encounter ignites her soul with hope. Amidst the darkness, a heartwarming Christmas tale of redemption and love unfolds, where faith can change even the hardest of hearts...

Turn the page and let's begin

❄

CHAPTER 1

❄

Manchester, England
Angel Street - September 1877

Georgina followed Paddy Slobcrude over the cobblestones of Angel Street, her frayed dress clinging to her damp skin. Her mood mirrored the gloomy, overcast skies above the desolate, rain-soaked slums of Manchester. Paddy predicted rain all day, and Georgina was convinced it would persist in her thoughts as well.

She hated working out in the rain and that coupled with the presence of Paddy, made this into another horrible day; one she could simply add to her ever-growing list of dreadful days.

Paddy was a brute. A merciless taskmaster with a foul mouth, a breath that smelled like the cheap liquor he drank, an odor barely masking the stench of his rotten teeth, and a hand that could deliver a stinging blow in all the wrong places.

She had little choice, though. She was only ten, and this was life. The only life she'd ever seen and according to Uncle Doyle, it would always stay this way. Nobody could ever do anything about it. Uncle Doyle said so, and he knew everything. At least, so he said.

He made the rules and whatever he said was the truth. And one of those truths was that she needed to cooperate with Paddy Slobcrude.

Uncle had made a deal with Paddy. The smelly, foul fiend with his snake eyes could borrow her for a day or two on days Uncle did not feel like going out. Then Paddy could use her to steal and cheat, something she was very good at. Much better than Uncle and Paddy.

Paddy Slobcrude practically lived in the same alley, just one shack further down, and on those days that she'd steal for Paddy, Uncle, of course, got a hefty part of the loot. That was the deal. Georgina got nothing other than a shove in the back, a bowl of watery soup, and a string of curses.

Paddy wanted her to call him *Mister* Paddy. That made him feel important, or something like that.

But he was anything but important. Just a low-life, a disgraceful, vile character who did not know the meaning of kindness. He was like a brute beast, created to be destroyed; a sinner without understanding whose mind had been darkened. Not that she understood what that meant, but it somehow sounded just like *Mister* Paddy. She had once heard that from a gibface who was screaming out loud to a group of bystanders while standing on a wiggly soap-box. The fellow was waving an outstretched finger in the air and then brought down his fist in his other hand while shouting ominous curses about some place with a fire where you'd burn forever and even longer. Some bystander told her he was a street-preacher, a Bible-basher. She had not liked him, but that thing about brute beasts had stayed with her. It sounded just about right, although in some ways, Paddy was not just having his understanding darkened; he was just plain dumb. The fool had not the faintest idea how to lift someone's purse, and if it had not been for Uncle Doyle farming her out, Paddy would have died years ago in the poorhouse from lack of food in his oversized beer belly.

Paddy stopped.

He was standing right in a puddle and nodded into the far distance to what appeared to be a couple seeking shelter from the rain under a large chestnut tree, right on Factory Street.

"What?" Georgina asked as she looked at Paddy. She knew there was a large hole in the sole of his boot. No doubt his socks, if he even had any, were soaked. Maybe he would catch pneumonia. That would make the world a better place.

"You see them," he hissed through his teeth. "Why don't you try them? They have money."

Georgina stared through the drizzling fog and saw them. A man and a woman. They were romantically involved. The man was gesticulating with his arm, telling the woman something, probably some drivel about her pretty eyelashes. Then his hand went up. He was clutching a walking cane and traced a semicircle in the air, as though illustrating the magnitude of the riches he would bestow upon her if she were to accept his proposals. Whatever stupidity he was telling her seemed to work, as the woman broke out in laughter.

Yes, they could stand to lose a few coins.

Often, stealing bothered Georgina. Especially when the folks she approached looked somewhat friendly. To steal from kind people was a lot harder than to steal from those hardened business men who looked at you as if you were just a piece of trash. Some people treated you like you were a mistake in God's production center, and God himself had handed you over to the garbage angels who were commanded to dump the mistakes upon earth. Stealing from those folks was always easier than lifting a purse from some woman who looked like she carried the weight of the world on her shoulders, or who actually appeared to be good.

Uncle Doyle said that such thoughts were ridiculous, as there were no truly kind people. At least, that's what Uncle Doyle said. "All people are bad", he said, "Except me and Paddy, and sometimes I even wonder about him." Once, when she'd told him she didn't actually like stealing, he told her it was normal to feel that way; at least in the beginning. "You get over those feelings real soon, Georgina," he said. "The first time I cheated on someone, I also felt a little weird, but I lost that feeling a long time ago. Gets better each time you fool someone and you'll learn soon enough you can count on nobody except yourself. One day, you'll be grateful I taught you those lessons."

Georgina figured she was a slow learner, because she'd been on the street for quite some time now, and she still could not get rid of that irritating, gnawing feeling of guilt when she deceived a friendly person. Her innocent blue eyes and her sweet demeanor always did the trick.

Of course, it was sort of fun too. When she unexpectedly ran off with someone's purse while curses and cries for help from the victim followed her like a swarm of angry bees, she felt nothing but a sense of victory with the adrenaline coursing through her body. Later, though, in the evening, while huddled on her straw mattress on the floor, images of her deceit would invariably return, and so did the questions. Was this really all that life was about? It seemed so senseless and it just didn't make her feel very good. But what could she do about it? Nothing; nothing at all. So, she decided it was best to push those sentiments and the annoying questions as far away as was possible and hope they would eventually just disappear.

"Well ... how about it?" Uncle Paddy snarled. "We haven't got all day." Georgina was abruptly snapped out of her reverie, and as Paddy sought refuge behind a mound of haphazardly discarded stones on the sidewalk, she approached her targets. They were completely absorbed in each other and had no regard for their surroundings. A fatal mistake, and she expected this job to be as easy as shooting a fish in a barrel.

She could do this.

When she came near the unsuspecting couple, she clenched her teeth, narrowed her eyes, and then slipped on the wet, glistening cobblestones. She uttered a coarse screech and fell face down onto the stones, breaking out into audible weeping. It looked real. Very real.

"Good Heavens dear." The woman cried out and her face registered horror. The man had just clasped his hands into those of the lady, but she swiftly disentangled and hurried towards Georgina, hoisting her high dress to safeguard it from the filth on the street. "The poor sheep fell," she lamented. "Oh, Taylor, we must help her."

Good. Everything goes as I planned.

Georgina had long ago learned that the best way to reach someone's heart was through pain and misfortune. A faultless young vagrant with a bloody knee and tacky smears of tears on her sunken face were typically enough to soften even the flintiest of hearts. The perfect trap for an unsuspecting victim.

As the lady approached and bent over Georgina, she sighed deeply and said, "Oh, my poor little girl. Does it hurt badly?"

Georgina stood up, crying, and stroked her elbow with a pained face. "Oh, ma'am, it hurts so much," she croaked and cast the lady a desperate stare. The lady beckoned to her male companion. "Taylor, come here. That poor child must have broken her arm. It doesn't look good."

Like a tomcat suddenly confronted by a bloodthirsty slobbering bulldog, Taylor recoiled, and his blissful, friendly expression turned into a grimace of reluctance.

Not one of the kind ones, Georgina thought. *That makes it easier.*

"That's a street kid," the man who was called Taylor scorned. "That one is full of lice and you shouldn't touch it."

It? I am a human being, Mister. I'll show you a thing or two.

Georgina was cunning. And smart. In spite of everything that was going on, she had her eyes wide open and spotted every detail that was worth noticing. The lady had a beautiful bracelet that sparkled even though the sky was cloudy and dark. The man wore a stylish suit and a deftly top hat adorned his rather lumpish face. She noticed how his hand slipped into the pocket of his coat and clasped something there. That might be a money pouch.

But Taylor seemed to be of the School of Saint Thomas. He narrowed his eyes and gave her a foul stare. Did he smell a rat? Georgina's thoughts darted through her head. She had to decide quickly whether she would try to snatch the dazzling bracelet or take a shot at Taylor's coat pocket.

The lady was kind, at least, she appeared to be.

The man was not.

It made the choice easy. She'd go for the man's pocket.

She squeezed out a few more tears from the corners of her eyes and asked in a small voice, "Do you really think it's broken? Oh, ma'am, that would be so bad. I am a beggar girl and need to bring in the money for my sick mother."

The lady was completely duped, and her defenses were down. Georgina had done her work well. "Taylor!" she demanded. "Come here and look at this poor young girl. You are a physician, for crying out loud."

Taylor hesitated. He kept at a distance.

"I-I can't feel my fingers anymore," Georgina cried out in alarm, and accompanied her new discovery with another wail of terror.

That did wonders.

The lady turned and rudely pulled Taylor by the arm that was stuck in his pocket. "Do something, Taylor. Show me some courage," the woman cried. "What was it you told me the other day about that oath you had to swear, that oath of Hippopotamus?"

"Hippocrates, dear," Taylor replied while wrinkling his nose. "It's called the oath of Hippocrates."

"Whatever," the lady hissed. She was clearly getting annoyed with her friend. "Show me you are worth your salt."

"But Angelique ... I...,"

"Taylor, now!"

He obeyed. When Georgina heard the commanding tone in Angelique's voice, she knew Taylor would surrender. If he did not, his chances of romance would be hopelessly skewed. And thus, she saw his coat pocket coming closer and closer. He no longer kept his hand in his pocket. His priceless possession was not guarded and would be an easy prey. It was a gamble. She had no way of knowing what it was he kept in his pocket, but it looked promising. Uncle Doyle always said, "Every theft is a gamble."

"Show me your arm, little girl," he said with a hint of irritation.

"I can't move it properly, Sir," Georgina peeped. "It must be broken for sure."

"Of course not, girl," he huffed. "You are young. Your bones aren't brittle as those of an old lady."

He was now very close. Georgina could smell his pomade. Nice, but not nice enough to not go through with her little deception.

"Can't you see the little lamb is hurting, Taylor," Angelique scoffed. "I thought you were different."

"I am not, dear ... It's just that this girl — "

This was Georgina's chance. Taylor was reaching forward. The smell of the pomade became stronger, and his pocket was within easy reach. She was as swift as lightning and in one fast move, just before Taylor put his gloved hand on her shoulder, her hand disappeared into his coat pocket, felt something, grabbed it, and pulled it out. With her arm that was supposedly broken, she gave the Taylor person a sharp push, and the startled man moved back.

She heard the lady let out a scream, and Taylor cursed.

Run Georgina ... Run. You must run.

This was the best part. She'd done this a thousand times, but every time it was a rush. The feeling of danger, of doing something exciting, of walking the fine line ... It was the only thing about this whole endeavor that made any sense.

And so, she ran as fast as her legs could carry her while clasping her loot. Away from Factory Street, and into the myriad of tiny, broken-down alleys of the Manchester slums. Not even the police knew their way around here, but she did. She would never get caught.

After she'd run for ten minutes, she allowed herself a break. Panting and sighing, she leaned against a rough wall, surrounded by mud and dirt. A couple of fat rats, clearly the inhabitants of this alley, glared at her with their vicious, beady eyes. But they were not the ones to watch out for. She pricked up her ears and listened for any sounds that showed they were after her. Nothing. Nobody followed her and there were not even garbled screams for help. It had been a perfect theft again.

She looked around to see if there was anybody else watching her, beside the rats. When she was certain there was no one around, she opened her hand and looked. A money bag indeed. She'd been right. Her gamble had been profitable. The bag was closed with a leather string. When she poured out the contents onto her open palm, she gasped. No coins to speak of, but there was a shiny ring with a precious stone attached to it. Was it a marriage ring that Taylor was about to give to the woman?

However, her excitement quickly waned when she thought about what would happen next. The ring would make both Uncle Doyle and Paddy happy, but had it been worth it? She'd get her bowl of watery soup and no doubt another scolding. Worse was that annoying feeling that crept up once again. The woman had been kind, and there was a possibility she had purloined a wedding ring that

Taylor was just about to present as a symbol of his affection. He had been an arrogant fobdoodle still … it didn't feel good. She shrugged her shoulders and tried to shake it off, and began finding her way to the appointed meeting place where she would hand the money pouch over to Paddy.

There was nothing else to do.

Nothing else to expect.

She had not been attracted to that street-preacher on his soap box who had been screaming fire and brimstone, but would it not be nice if there was a God? A loving God, as she had heard someone else say, who cared for you and watched over you?

But if there was, he surely would want nothing to do with her. She was as black and as foul as they came and from what she had gathered, heaven was a place for the good people; the land where everyone was lovely and pure. No way she would get in.

As she pondered these things, she thought again of the words Uncle Doyle had uttered. "All religion is a lie to force people to follow the rules of the rich." He had looked especially foul when he told her she should never, ever have anything to do with God. While wiping the drops of liquor off his lips with his grubby hands, he hissed, "The only business in this world that's more profitable than stealing is religion, and I would add that stealing is not nearly so corrupt."

Uncle Doyle could know. He knew everything and always spoke the truth.

At least, that's what he said…

CHAPTER 2

❄

Manchester, England
Simeon Street - December 1883

"What do you mean, you don't like Christmas?" Danyell Simmons asked. "Everybody likes Christmas." He narrowed his eyes at Georgina with an expression of skepticism, as if she had just claimed that the moon was made of fresh cheese. "What is there not to like? People are nice at Christmas time, there are lights everywhere, beautiful songs, good food, and I usually get a set of new clothes."

"Well, I don't," Georgina snapped back and defiantly stared back into Danyell's eyes. "I don't get new clothes at Christmas. The people I know are not nice, and Uncle Doyle's cuisine is never good at Christmas. The fact is, the food I eat is never edible. Not during Christmas and not anywhere else in the year."

"Never?" Danyell's eyes grew wide.

"Never," Georgina replied. As she looked at Danyell, his amazement almost made her feel good. At least she had something that caused him to wonder. She cleared her throat and said, "I've heard people talk about the magic of Christmas; nonsense about peace on earth and good will to all men, but two days after Christmas, the streets are just as cold and hostile as they were on the day before Christmas." She shivered. The wind was cold and icy and the muffin man predicted snow. "There's no peace on earth, at least not in our street."

"Your Uncle still beating you?"

"He does."

Danyell rubbed the back of his neck. "You shouldn't let him. How old are you now?"

A blush appeared on her face. She was no child. She could fend for herself. Without looking at him, she mumbled, "I am sixteen."

Danyell let out a whistle. "Wow. Sixteen. That means I am only one year older than you are. Trust me, it's time you get away from your uncle."

"That's easy for you to say," Georgina said. "You've got a wonderful home, with parents that care for you. I have only Uncle Doyle. That's not the same."

"Where are your parents?"

"Dead."

"I am sorry."

Georgina looked up and swallowed hard. "Don't be. I never knew them. My father and my mother got killed while robbing a store. That's why Uncle Doyle is taking care of me. He's my father's brother."

"He's *not* taking care of you. He's an evil man."

"Everyone is evil, except…" She stopped. She had wanted to say, except you, but that was a stupid thing to say, and maybe it wasn't even true. She hardly knew Danyell.

Danyell's shoulders drooped. "Not everyone is evil. That's not true. Who told you that?"

"Uncle Doyle did."

A chuckle escaped Danyell's throat. "Of course, Uncle Doyle. Do you even hear what you're saying?" His stare narrowed, and he looked right at her. An uncomfortable stare. "There are lots of good, God-fearing people. You just haven't met them yet." He hesitated and then added in a conspiratorial whisper, "If I were you, I'd run away. Today rather than tomorrow."

Georgina cast him an angry glance. "Sure, Mister Know It All. And where would I go?" Before Danyell could answer, she added, "I don't like this conversation. If you insist on talking about me, I'll go somewhere else."

"No, no." He stated. His nose twitched. "I didn't mean to be so inquisitive. We were just talking about Christmas."

"Right," Georgina said. "You were saying how nice Christmas is. But just so you know, I have no special lights, no hot meal, and no Christmas songs around some open fire, although…" There was a hint of a smile on her face.

"What?"

"… I am actually glad there's no singing in our house. If Uncle would sing, it would make our place even more unbearable than it already is."

Danyell shook his head. "But you do like singing?"

"I don't know." She shuffled her broken left shoe over the rough pavement. "I guess I do like music, but I've never heard much. And … as far as singing, I've never learned how."

Danyell raised his hand as if to stop Georgina from speaking. "That can't be true," he said. "Everybody knows how to sing. Everybody likes music, even street girls like you."

Street girls, like me? His words stung. Even though he was right, she couldn't stand it when someone shoved her nose into the facts. But that was all she was, a street girl. He was wrong though, about everybody being able to sing. She'd never sung, and as far as she could see, she never would.

Danyell seemed oblivious to the hurt in Georgina's eyes, and his face lit up as though he had just thought of something.

"Come by my father's store this afternoon. I'll get you something."

Georgina raised her brow and offered Danyell a questioning gaze. He was nice, although a little strange, in believing the world harbored good people. But what if he were right, and there were nice people, friends she had never yet met? Danyell was just about the only one who actually stopped to talk to her and that while he belonged to a better class. That was rare. People better situated never stopped to talk to her. They only talked to her when she was about to relieve them of their purse. But Danyell didn't have a purse that was worth stealing, and even if he did, she would not want to take it. He was one of the few good ones. Of course, Uncle did not agree and wanted to steal from him. Danyell's father ran a profitable grocery store, and once Danyell had given her a whole sausage for free and that with no particular motive. When she handed the sausage to Uncle, his eyes became greedy, as if he were a fly who had discovered a fresh batch of cow dung, and he right away came up with a plan to rob the store. She should have never given the sausage to Uncle, but eaten it herself. "Act ever so friendly; get in that kid's dad's good graces, find out where he keeps his money, and make a run for it."

No-No-No. A thousand times, no. She would not do it. She had stood her ground, had gotten a good beating for it, and Uncle, in his fury, had immediately farmed her out to Paddy Slobcrude for the entire week. But no, she would not steal from Danyell or his father.

She looked up at Danyell and tilted her head. "Come by the store? Do you have a sausage for me like last time?"

He pursed his lips. "Sure, I can get you another sausage, if you like. I'll ask my Pa, but I was thinking of something else."

A Christmas present perhaps?

A peculiar sense of warmth radiated through Georgina's body. Nobody had ever given her a real present; not for her birthday and not for Christmas. "Let me guess ... you have a Christmas present for me?"

Danyell shook his head. "Not quite; after all, it's not Christmas yet. But I am sure you'll like it. And it carries a bit of the Christmas spirit too."

"What time shall I be at the store?"

"Just before my father closes."

"That's late. Uncle Doyle wants me home before dark. He says the riff-raff comes out after dark."

"Does he now?" Danyell croaked. "Don't worry. There will be no such people where we are going. And it's my guess the sausage will pacify your uncle."

That was true. The warm feeling that had risen in her heart was still there. Bringing home meat would bring a rare moment of joy to their dismal hovel. The scent of smoked pork would fill the air and light up her uncle's greedy, puckered face. Even though today had been bad and she had pilfered nobody's purse yet, the sausage would make the evening bearable.

"I'll be there," she said.

"Good. Remember, my father closes the store right when the clock strikes six. Don't be late."

"I won't," Georgina said and she could not hide the grin on her face. If she had known a song, any song, she would have hummed it right then.

❄

Danyell's father worked in a better neighborhood. Not an area Georgina often went to. While most people here were obviously well-to-do, which made them tempting targets, the chances of getting caught were much higher, too. There were a lot more police around, and she definitely stood out in her ragged and unkempt appearance. She'd gotten caught here once. That had been years ago, and of course, it had all been *Mister* Paddy's fault. He'd pushed her to steal from an aging gentleman who was out on a walk with his grandson. She had not liked the fierce dog that trailed behind them. While she liked dogs, and usually befriended most of them with no difficulty, this dog had been different. He'd scared her with menacing eyes, and she had not wanted to approach the man. Paddy, as usual, couldn't care less and forced her to approach the man with his grandchild and the slobbering dog anyway.

It went wrong. Paddy escaped, she did not.

Dogs have a sixth sense and this dog knew she was up to no good. As soon as she came near them and had just begun her routine of deception, all hell broke loose. The salivating creature forcefully grabbed her arm the instant her hand made contact with the gentleman's pocket. It didn't really bite, but wouldn't let go either. Spending a night in a rat-infested cell at the police station was the result. There, she had to withstand a severe beating from a fat officer who claimed to possess expertise in disciplining individuals like her. Thank you, Paddy.

It was the last time she'd ever tried her luck in this part of Manchester. Nevertheless, Danyell's father's store was not hard to find and when the Manchester Cathedral rang its loud and deafening bell, and told the entire city it was six o'clock, she arrived. She hid near a tree while keeping her eyes glued to the door of the shop.

It was already dark, and Georgina shivered. She was not used to being out this late and the wind was biting cold. Whatever Danyell had cooked up for her, it better be worth it. The air smelled differently here. Where Georgina lived, the air was permeated with the pungent tang of the nearby tannery and when the wind came in from the wrong direction, the smoke from the wretched place was so thick it seemed to swallow up entire parts of the street. But not here. Even though the horse manure seemed as bountiful as anywhere else in the city, the air smelled fresher. In the distance, she could see the street-lighter at work. He skilfully lit one gaslight after the other, and he'd soon lit the lantern near the store as well.

She stared at the flickering streetlights. They almost looked pretty, and if it had not been so cold, she would have enjoyed the scenery. *Come on, Danyell. I am freezing.*

There he was. The front door of the store opened and Danyell appeared. He was carrying something in his arms, and Georgina tilted her head to get a better look. She gasped as she saw he also carried an enormous sausage that dangled at his side.

"I am over here. Danyell," she cried out as she moved away from her shadowy hiding place.

When he spotted her, he swung the sausage in the air, as if to show he'd kept his promise and walked over to her.

"Right on time," he said when he neared. "Let's go. They start soon."

"Who is starting and where are we going? Are we going to pick up my Christmas present?"

"So many questions at once," Danyell replied, his face carrying a mysterious grin. "Remember, I told you it's not Christmas yet. But I've got your sausage. Look how large a one. I was surprised my father was willing to part with this banger."

Georgina nodded. Getting such a gift was rare. "Will you hold on to it for now?" she timidly asked. "If people see me carrying such a delightful piece of meat, they'll surely think I stole it."

"You carry it," he said with a chuckle. "You can hide it under your coat."

"My coat? I don't have a coat."

"You do now," Danyell cheered, and with one swing of his arm, he revealed a brown jacket with fur around the cuffs and neck. He had kept it hidden behind his back. "You need a jacket. I can't see how you can stand being out on the streets without a jacket."

Georgina blinked her eyes and stared at it in bewilderment. "I-Is it for me?" she said at last.

"If you'll have it. It's a boy's coat, really. It used to be my skating jacket, but it's way too small for me." He pushed it into Georgina's hands. She let her fingers slide over the fur. "I-Is it real fur?"

He shrugged. "Think so. You really don't mind it's not a girl's jacket?"

"Do I mind?" Georgina shook her head. "Of course not. It's the loveliest thing I've ever seen"

"Then put it on. We have to hurry. They start soon."

Georgina felt as if heaven had come down. Never before had anybody ever given her anything, let alone a precious, priceless gift like a coat. Still, she hesitated. Could she accept something so costly as a coat? "Will your father be mad?" she asked at last. "He may have wanted to sell it for a good price."

"It's fine," Danyell muttered. "He was the one who suggested it when I asked him about the sausage."

"He did?" Georgina couldn't believe her ears. Why would someone give something as precious as a coat to a street-girl like she was? Was Danyell's father a saint or something? She studied Danyell's eyes for a moment, even though it was hard to see his expression in the shimmering light, but something told her it was really true and the coat was hers to keep. She slid in her left arm, then her right one, and then pulled the coat over her shoulders. The fur touched her neck. It was the loveliest feeling she'd ever felt.

"There's a bit of a scent," Danyell explained. "Mothballs. I hate those things."

Georgina smelled nothing bad. Everything about this jacked was just wonderful. It was warm, comfortable, and to her, it carried the scent of heaven. "How do I look?" she inquired as she paraded a few steps before Danyell.

He pressed his lips together. "A bit too small for you, but I've got no other coat. I suppose it will have to do."

"It's so lovely," Georgina replied. "It's the very best thing that ever happened to me."

Danyell nodded. "You'll be needing it tonight. You need to look at least a little presentable. Now, take your sausage and hide it under your coat. We've got to go." He handed her the meat and, without waiting for her reply, walked off.

Georgina flew after him. She was walking on air.

They crossed the street, took a left turn, then a right, and suddenly they stood in front of the magnificent Manchester Cathedral. A row of gas lanterns cast a mysterious, fairy-tale glow over the stone walls with their pointed turrets and beautiful stained-glass windows.

"A-Are we going inside?" Georgina asked.

He paused and stole her a quick glance. "Not in the main cathedral. We'll go to a place on the side. It's used for smaller services, as the Cathedral itself is way too big for simple services and activities." He pointed to something Georgina could not discern in the shimmering lights. "Over there."

Georgina felt a flutter in her heart as she stared upon the colossal structure in front of her and exhaled a deep breath.

"Ever been inside the cathedral itself?" Danyell asked. "It's beautiful."

Georgina felt a blush on her face. "Inside? Never. That's no place for a girl like me."

He let out a chuckle. "Of course, it is; it's God's house. Everyone is welcome there. But, as I said, tonight we won't go in the main part. Just follow me."

As they came closer, Georgina felt like she was shrinking with every step she took. The stately cathedral seemed to rise in size proportionally. She had heard about the beauty of the Manchester Cathedral. It had been erected hundreds of years before; it survived a thousand and one wars. Kings had visited the place and important rich folks had knelt there before the altar. But, most importantly, it was the house in which God, in whom she did not believe, lived; together with all the singing angels. There were rumors circulating on the streets that within the grand edifice, there was a door to paradise, provided you were privy to its location. She would never know. People like herself were not allowed inside.

And why would she even want to search for such a door? God didn't exist.

At home, in Uncle's chilly hovel, where the wind blew mercilessly through the dirty, broken windows and the cracks in the walls, and where she was barely given anything decent to eat, the thought of a loving God who cared for your every need seemed ridiculous. It was one of the few things Uncle Doyle may have been correct about.

But now, facing the grandeur of the cathedral, she wasn't so sure anymore he had it right. Walking towards the holy of holiest in a warm, new coat, while clutching a sausage to her breast together with someone she could actually call a friend, made her tremble in reverence. All of Uncle Doyle's cutting, mocking words about religion seemed empty and void of understanding. It sure seemed like some higher power was shining favorably on her today.

As they approached the towering oak doors that granted access to the holy sanctuary, Danyell suddenly swerved left and gestured for her to join him. "To the other door, remember?"

It was then she noticed they were not alone. Many other people, some looking very distinguished and wealthy, were walking along the same path and were apparently all going to the same place. There was even a couple with three cute little children. Georgina felt her cheeks getting warm as she noticed the boy who must not have been older than eight or nine. He was wearing almost an exact copy of her own coat. She moved to the side and walked as far out of sight as was possible.

"There we go in," Danyell whispered and nodded with his head towards a side-building. Not nearly as impressive as the cathedral itself, but still a part of the glorious overall structure. The door was open. An older, balding fellow stood at the entrance, carrying a large grin. He made a small bow and beamed such an enormous smile to everyone that it prompted Georgina to wonder whether he knew each individual on a personal level.

"Who is that?" she whispered as she inconspicuously pointed a finger at him.

"That? Oh, that's Bartholomew Brooke. He's the caretaker. Not of the main cathedral, but he oversees this place; sometimes he helps with the sermons. Sort of like an assistant pastor."

Sermons like the fellow on the wobbly soap-box? Georgina felt a slight shiver, but bravely followed Danyell. Even though this building was a part of the main cathedral, it looked not nearly as impressive. That was good. She had no business in that impressive other structure where God ruled. That was just too hot a place to be. Surely, God himself lived there, and would be guarding that special door to heaven with the eye of an eagle, in a holy effort to prevent misfits like herself from slipping by unnoticed.

Still, the place where they were about to enter looked impressive as well. Above the open door was a beautiful stained glass window depicting a cross on a hill, and the architect had embellished the edge of the slanted roof with a couple of pointed spires adorned with tiny windows. Who'd be living there?

"Here it is," Danyell whispered, "This is my surprise to you. It's music night. There's a brass band and I believe you will hear some beautiful singing too. You told me you know nothing about music … well, that's about to change." A grand smile adorned his face and he stepped forward to go inside.

In front of them in the queue of people waiting to enter was a stout, rather chubby man. He was neatly dressed in a tight suit and a top hat that protected his wavy curls from the snow that had just begun to fall. His walking cane was decorated with a beautiful, sparkling stone. Impressive. A wealthy fellow indeed. He glanced casually at Danyell and then seemed to recognize him. He nodded encouragingly and spoke in a warm voice. "So, Danyell, nice seeing you." Then his eye fell on Georgina. He frowned and said, "And who do we have here? A friend of yours?"

"Yes, Sir," Danyell replied, not in the least perturbed. "This is Georgina Castle."

"Georgina huh?"

Georgina felt his eyes scrutinizing her and knew her cheeks were getting hot. The man tapped his cane on the cobble stones as if he were a general who inspected the troops and demanded everyone's attention. "A girl in boys' clothes, or a boy in girl's clothes?"

Georgina wanted to crawl under the pavement, but there was nowhere to hide, so she looked up and said in a small voice, "Hello, Sir. I am a girl. Just got this coat from Danyell."

"Did you now?" he said and frowned. Then thought better of it. He gave Danyell a light pat on the shoulder and muttered, "That was a mighty nice thing of you, Danyell. A very Christian thing." He turned again to Georgina and said, not in unfriendly tones, "Well, child, I hope you will enjoy the music as much as I will. You know, my son is singing tonight. You should hear him ... William is very good." After these words, he turned and walked on. He was now just moments away from reaching the vicar, who was about to immerse him in the comforting glow of his delighted smile.

And that's when everything changed.

Suddenly, Georgina caught a glimpse; a terrible glimpse of a ragged, unshaven, dirty face; a face she knew all too well. It was the ugly mug of Paddy Slobcrude.

What in the world was he doing here? Surely, the fiend didn't come for the music. There was only one reason why he was here... He came to steal, and he had his eyes on the sparkling cane of the gentleman standing before her.

CHAPTER 3

❄

Georgina wanted to shout and alert anyone within earshot that Paddy Slobcrude was here; a thief on the prowl. This night should not be disturbed by a ripple of evil, stirred up by the likes of Paddy Slobcrude or Uncle Doyle. Not tonight. Not on this evening when life seemed to finally smile on her ... But no sound escaped her lips. Instead, she grabbed Danyell's hand and squeezed it so hard, he softly yelped.

"What?" he grunted and cast her an irritated look. But it was too late.

Paddy, with sunken and bloodshot eyes was unable to restrain himself. The rascal stared hungrily at the cane of the wealthy man in line before them, and Georgina knew what was about to happen. By the looks of it, the rascal had hardly eaten anything for days. Of course, he had not. He was as skilled a thief as Queen Victoria was a rugby player. The sight of the cane, studded with the sparkling stone, spurred him into action. He charged towards the cane, swiftly seized it from the clutches of the plump man, who emitted a startled scream. She had never known Paddy to be fast, but he outdid himself as he disappeared around a corner. What desperate hunger can do to a man.

"Help," the man cried. "A thief ... There's a thief in the crowd."

Pandemonium broke loose. People gasped, others shouted curses while checking their pockets, and women screamed in fear. But a few youngsters kept their cool and were not carried away by the wave of dismay and confusion that poured over all. They gave chase.

Bad luck for Paddy, because the gaunt heap of misery, in spite of his surprise attack, was no match for the well-practiced and muscular boys. After only a short distance, the boys were on top of Paddy and threw him to the ground. They dragged him back to his feet, his hands gripped tightly in theirs, and rudely pushed him back to the scene of his crime. All the while, Paddy's curses filled the air. The onlookers waved their fists, spat on him, and yelled curses back at Paddy.

Georgina almost felt sorry for him. But not for long, for he spotted her in the crowd and when their eyes locked it was disturbing. She shivered. Looking into his eyes was like gazing into an ocean of darkness, devoid of affection and with no notion of morality. If you'd fall into it, you would wake up in a world composed of hell's pitch-black tar, where demons would be your only companions. Not good. Not good at all. Why had she never seen this?

While still looking at her, suddenly he cried out, "She made me do it." He savagely pointed with his head to Georgina. "She and her uncle. They are the real crooks here. I am only hired to do their dirty work."

Georgina froze. *What is he talking about?*

But as she felt the eyes of countless people turned on her, panic rose. Her first reaction was to run. She had to get away from here. While she had nothing to do with Paddy's crime, her many years on the street had taught her that justice does not apply to a street girl. Her lips began to tremble, and she felt her muscles tense.

"There," Paddy cried out again, "Look! It's the girl in that stupid boy's coat."

Why was he doing that? Suddenly, it was as if a thousand fingers pointed at her and even as many voices shouted a terrible verdict: "Guilty. Guilty. Guilty."

Should she run into Manchester Cathedral and find sanctuary or the door to heaven and so escape the horrors of this world?

Of course, she could not. God, who didn't even exist, would be the first to shout out her guilt, even though she was not guilty. At least, not of Paddy's crime. But she was plenty guilty of a thousand other thefts.

"Have mercy on my soul," she cried out. "I had nothing to do with this." But it was hopeless and she could tell nobody believed her.

That's when she ran.

She turned around in a blind daze of panic and stormed off. Something fell and blocked her step. It almost made her stumble. She realized in a flash it was her sausage. She had forgotten about her prize gift and the thing now rolled over on the ground. It caused more gasps and screams from the onlookers. "There is the proof. She stole a sausage. Get her!" as it was obvious to all that she had stolen it.

She had to get away. She pushed someone aside, kicked another person, crashed into a woman, and then a strong, firm hand grabbed her by the neck. "Not so fast, young lady," an angry, dark male voice spoke near her ear. While continuing to kick and fight like a cat they forcibly tried to plunge into freezing water, another pair of hands grasped her legs. She was lifted off the ground and hoisted back to the entrance of the building where everyone was shouting and yelling obscenities right in front of the house of God.

Thank goodness, there was Danyell.

His face was ashen white, and he helplessly lifted both hands in the air. "A mistake," he cried. "She had nothing to do with it. I invited her to come with me."

The wealthy man whose cane had been snatched stared at him with a doubtful expression. He had retrieved his cane and pounded it aggressively on the pavement. "Maybe she fooled you, young man. I know her type. These thieves are terribly cunning."

Guilty, guilty, guilty....

The words guilty kept ringing in Georgina's ears like the monotone chant from some spooky monks from the netherworld who were preparing some sort of sacrifice.

Danyell was now shouting at the top of his lungs. "She did nothing. Let go of her. You all saw that other fellow snatching the cane."

The other fellow?

A fresh wave of normalcy washed over the crowd. The other fellow had done it. That was true. They first needed to deal with the other fellow. All eyes turned and looked at the place where they had last seen the thief. But no more. Paddy was gone. In all the confusion, he had diverted the attention from his catchers and ran off.

The two youngsters stared dumbfounded at each other, resembling two puppy dogs who had been caught chewing their master's gold-threaded slippers. "W-Where did he go?" the one stammered to the other.

"I thought you held him," came the weak reply that sounded more like an accusation than a question.

A constable approached, a peeler whose belly had absorbed more ale than was good for him. He glanced for a moment at Georgina and motioned for the two men holding her they could put her down. They did, but kept holding on to her, not wanting to make the same mistake as the other fellows had made. Danyell ran up to her, his face full of concern.

The constable walked up to the man with the cane. "I am so sorry, Mister Russell. Is it true that this girl stole nothing?" The cane man, whose name was apparently Mister Russell, gave Georgina a hard stare that seemed to last for an uncomfortable, long while. At last, he shrugged his shoulders and while shaking his head, he muttered, "Thank you, Constable Crowley, no, she did not."

Georgina heaved a sigh of relief and felt the hands of the men who had held her, loosen. Danyell leaned towards her and whispered, "Mister Russell is an important man in Manchester who donates much to the church. His son sings in the choir."

Whatever he was or was not did not interest Georgina. She wanted to get away from this horrible place. Her night was ruined. The whole scene had deeply hurt and humiliated her. Now she had to go back to her horrible hovel without her sausage and face an angry and unreasonable Uncle Doyle.

The fat constable stepped up, positioned himself before her, leaned his angry face forward, and raised his shoulders as high as he could in the hopes of looking impressive and scary, as if he were the top dog around, whose job it was to keep all the little mongrels of the street toeing the line. But Georgina was not about to be cowered into submission by the fat constable and his slobbering jaws for something she had not done. She gave him a defiant stare and said, "What?"

He towered over her while narrowing his eyes, but hesitated, almost as if he were contemplating whether or not that little street dog in front of him was capable of delivering a snappy bite that would hurt his pride and would make him look stupid in the eyes of all the bystanders.

"My name is Constable Crowley and I am the law," he said, in an authoritative voice. "It seems this time you are innocent, but I know the likes of you. Trust me, your face has been imprinted on my memory. If I ever catch you for so much as just to be standing near one of these decent people here, I'll send you to Manchester prison."

You'll first have to catch me, Georgina thought, but decided to not make matters worse. She forced a humble, penitent sort of look on her face and gave him a nod. "Certainly, sure, Sir."

The constable, pleased his appearance had apparently made an impression, gave her a slight nod and added, "I don't know why you are here, but this is no place for a girl like you. Tonight, there's a concert for decent people, so I advise you to make yourself scarce and move out of here as fast as you can."

Danyell spoke up, still trying to solve the situation. "I invited her, constable. My father gave her the sausage, and I wanted her to hear some beautiful music."

"Sorry," the constable stated in a firm voice that left little doubt about what he wanted Georgina to do. "This is no place for her."

Danyell flashed Georgina a desperate glance. "I am so sorry to have brought you here, Georgina. I'll walk you home."

She shook her head. "I don't want you to, Danyell. I want to be alone."

The bystanders all hummed their agreement. Danyell understood, pressed his lips together and said, "So sorry, Georgina. I'll be seeing you around. At least, you got the coat, so all is not lost."

The coat? All was not lost?

Tears had never been readily shed by Georgina, but now she sensed the dam was on the verge of collapsing and she had to make a swift exit. Tears would make her humiliation complete. She would not cry in front of all these people.

"Thank you, Danyell," she muttered as she turned around and walked off.

Tomorrow, she would get back at all of them.

Tomorrow, she would be more relentless in her stealing...

All of these people would feel the wrath of her indignation, including that fat constable, Mister Russell with that stupid cane, and that silly vicar with his everlasting smile... she would rob them all.

Anger helped. The hardening of her heart always kept her from getting overly emotional, and this time it would be no different.

But this time it *was* different. A strange, unfamiliar sense of brokenness invaded her heart. It made her feel helpless, lonely, even hopeless, and as she made her way through the crowd, the first tears rolled over her cheeks. Hardening her heart didn't help this time and her angry, dark thoughts were being replaced by that horrible, monotonous chant of those monks again. *Guilty, guilty, guilty.*

Deep in her heart, she knew stealing from all these folks wouldn't make it better. But what would?

Just as she turned the corner, aimlessly marching ahead, she still heard the constable shout: "All right, everyone. The party is over. Let's get inside the church for some heartwarming music that will touch our heartstrings and will make us think of a better world, instead of our present one, so filled with devils and demons."

A world filled with devils and demons?

His words caused another tear to roll over Georgina's cheeks. Perhaps the constable was right, she was nothing but a miserable street girl; but a devil or a demon? That sounded bad. Surely that man could not have been talking about her, or … had he?

She needed to think about these matters, and tonight was a good night for it; all alone on the streets of Manchester. She would not go home tonight. In fact, maybe she would never go back to that miserable place. The idea of breaking away from Uncle Doyle was an exciting thought, even though it was an intensely silly one. She had no other place to go and nobody would take care of her.

Yet sorting out puzzling questions about who she was and what she needed to do in life, was better done on the lonely streets than in Uncle's place. And, come to think of it, if ever demons and devils did exist, then it was there in that mudhole of gloom and doom under the supervision of Uncle Doyle.

No, she was done going back there. No more beatings and humiliations when she had not pilfered enough coins. She no longer wanted to be farmed out to the likes of Mister Paddy … That rat who used her to make his own escape. It would be hard, it would be cold and almost impossible, but from now on she'd be on her own, and make her own choices. She could steal enough to keep herself alive and in the new jacket she had gotten from Danyell, she'd be as warm as on the floor in Uncle's place.

The thought of not returning to Uncle Doyle's place cheered her considerably. She still sniffed a few tears away, and even though the night had never looked darker than it did just then, she felt the peculiar sensation that somehow, a new dawn would be rising.

CHAPTER 4

❄

And so, Georgina walked. She had no idea where she was going. She'd never been in these parts of Manchester before and it appeared she was walking around in circles, as at one point she found herself again right in front of Manchester Cathedral, the house with the door to heaven. If only she could go in and find that door.

But of course, she could not. The massive oak doors in front of the cathedral were firmly closed. There was even an iron lock on the handle. If the cathedral had been open, she could have slipped in. Maybe she could do that tomorrow.

Could she? The place filled her with awe, but she had to stay somewhere. If she'd find out when the doors were open, she could somehow find her way in and hide somewhere, so she'd be safe for the night.

Would the music-night in the side-building already be over?

Couldn't hurt to find out, although she needed to be very careful, as she did not want to face that fat constable once more.

She followed the same way she and Danyell had walked earlier, and after a small while, she saw the side-building again.

Was that door open?

It was hard to see, as there was barely any light, but it looked like it stood open just a crack. Then she could go in. Her heart pounded as she considered going in. If the constable were to catch her, it would mean Manchester prison. That was a place to be avoided at all costs. She'd heard about it on the streets. Horrid tales of beatings and rats the size of fat cats, who would nibble on your toes when you dozed off alone in your cold, stony cell. No, better keep walking.

Although ... she could at least look. There was no law against looking if a door was open or closed, and if she'd be careful, nobody would catch her. And then, if indeed, the door was open she could sneak in. Finding a dark corner in a deserted hallway was a better prospect than walking around on the streets. Danyell's coat was wonderful, but it was getting cold... If she was to survive in her new life, she needed to take risks.

And so, she snuck through the shadows along the large walls of the cathedral towards the small building until she reached the door where only hours earlier, she had stood in anticipation of a most wonderful night while still clutching her sausage.

Open ... It was open. The door was open just a crack. Her breath stopped as she pushed it slightly with one hand. It creaked terribly, and she froze. If the constable was hiding behind a wall, he'd now come out and grab her by the neck.

Nobody came.

She waited another minute with bated breath and dared not to make a move. Finally, she relaxed and chuckled. Of course, there was no constable hiding in the freezing cold of the night. It was a silly thought. The man would be home long ago, probably sitting with his wife near an open fire while sipping hot chocolate milk, or, considering his belly, possibly something a bit more spirited.

The crack in the doorway had become large enough for her to squeeze through, and seconds later, she found herself in a dark hallway.

She let her eyes get adjusted to the darkness and began looking around for a warm place where she could lay her head. She moved forward until she came to another door. No doubt, there would be a large room behind it; possibly the place where they had their musical concert earlier. There she'd be warm and safe.

She let her hand slide over the rough wood until she felt the metal doorknob, large and cold.

Would it be locked?

She gave it a slight push, and the door opened halfway and without effort. To her relief, this door made no harrowing sound. But while the door had not creaked, there was another sound. What was it?

Careful, so as to not give herself away, she pushed the door open a little further and stuck her head in the next room. It was, as she had expected, a large room with benches all lined up and facing an altar. A grand candle that emitted its dancing light across the front illuminated the place in part and cast large, dancing shadows over the white, plastered walls.

Indeed, as Danyell had explained, a church.

Not nearly as grand and impressive as the cathedral next door, no doubt, but, nevertheless, a holy place. For a moment, Georgina stood mesmerized as she drank in the atmosphere of peace and sacredness. And then she saw where the sounds came from.

There, right next to the candle, stood a boy, or rather a young man, and he was singing.

She should have known somebody was there. Nobody would leave a church door unlocked on a cold wintry night in Manchester unless there was something going on.

She should run.

She needed to leave right quick.

But she did not. Instead, she listened to the singing. It was wonderful. She stood transfixed on the marble slabs of stone, entranced by the young man's song.

Safe in the arms of Jesus,
Safe on His gentle breast;
There by His love o'ershaded,
Sweetly my soul shall rest.
Hark! 'tis the voice of angels
Borne in a song to me,
Over the fields of glory,
Over the jasper sea.

The music lifted her away from her earthly plain so full of woes. It catapulted her into a sphere so serene that it felt like her heart was bursting with desire to unite with … with something wonderful; something outside of herself, something that was good, lovely, and kind.

Never before had Georgina heard something so pure. The young man, he couldn't be older than 17 or 18, had a wonderful voice, rich and deep and it resonated with such sincerity that Georgina could not move for fear of breaking the spell that had come over her. The words echoed around the walls of the church and although she did not understand what these words meant, she knew she witnessed something extraordinary, something that surpassed the beauty of the dark streets of Manchester, so filled with injustice, poverty, and horse manure.

Maybe the door to heaven was not at all in the cathedral, but it was here, in this small side-building, and she had stumbled upon it.

Jesus, my heart's dear Refuge,
Jesus has died for me;
Firm on the Rock of Ages
Ever my trust shall be.
Here let me wait with patience,
Wait till the night is o'er;
Wait till I see the morning
Break on the golden shore.

Those words were filled with such beauty and hope. She too, like the author of the song, was waiting until the night was over; until the dawn would break on a golden shore and she could leave her miserable life behind and walk through sun-streaked fields of hope and mercy.

Of course, that would never happen. It was the stuff that silly dreams were made of. And yet, the longing for such a place didn't feel silly at all.

The song was over.

The young man cleared his throat, looked at a paper he had laying on a table nearby, and prepared to start another song. At that moment, Georgina felt her throat itching. If she didn't do something quickly, she would burst out coughing and it would give away her presence. She fought the urge with all her might, but that only made matters worse. At last, she couldn't hold it in any longer and she broke out in a despicable coughing spell.

The young man looked up, startled.

He had seen her and looked in her direction.

"Pray tell, who doth approach?" he exclaimed from afar, his words resounding through the church.

"I-I ...," Georgina stammered, "I am sorry to be here." That was a stupid thing to say. She was not sorry at all. She had just heard the most beautiful thing she'd ever heard, but it was obvious she wasn't supposed to be here, and she was most sorry to have been caught.

"Don't be," the young man said. He climbed down from the stage and came her direction.

As he made his way forward, another urge welled up. *Run, girl. Run while you can.*

He was still quite some distance away, and if she'd be fast, she'd be safe. Then, he could do nothing bad to her. One encounter with ugly hands grabbing her legs and arms, one lecture from the fat constable, and that one threat of prison hanging over her head was enough for one evening. But, somehow, her feet refused to move, and she hesitated.

How could somebody that produced such loveliness be so mean and horrible as to call the constable? Neither did he look mean and evil. If the features of Uncle Doyle had been etched onto his face, she'd be long gone, but he did not resemble that man at all. Dressed in gray knickerbockers with a matching vest and jacket, he looked stylish, but nothing too fancy. Still, it betrayed a wealthy upbringing, and it was obvious he had nothing to do with a life on the streets. Best of all, he smiled, and she spotted no hint of frustration or anger on his youthful face. Thus, he approached with steady steps in his low-heeled dress shoes and a curious smile was plastered around his lips. "Who are you?" he asked, when he stopped before her and studied her intently. "I am William."

"My-My name is Georgina," she answered, and felt her face getting hot as she was able to perceive his attractive face in greater detail. A lovely face it was. His blue eyes sparkled with an intriguing glow. His supple chestnut locks were impeccably groomed and parted to the side.

Each hair seemed in place. Georgina's hand rose to arrange the disorder she knew was present on her own head. She was no match for this young man.

"Why are you here?"

"Me? I ... eh ...". Georgina stumbled over her words, feeling a bit faint. "I just heard your singing and wanted to listen. I am sorry to interrupt. It just sounded so lovely."

"You heard me singing?" An even broader grin emerged. "I am just practicing. I was singing here earlier tonight, but it didn't go as well as I had wanted it to, so I figured I could benefit from practicing a bit more, once the others had left."

"You sang here tonight for all the people?"

"I did. We had a musical evening here. Not just me singing. There were others too but overall, it was lovely. Yet, my father wasn't pleased. He said I could do better." He shrugged his shoulders. "I am glad you liked it."

"I did, I really did," Georgina said. "In fact, I never knew singing could be so nice."

He eyed her from the corner of his eyes. "You never heard much singing?"

"No, never." She lowered her glance and noticed the frayed edges of her broken shoes. What would William think of her? She just looked so awful.

"It's nicer with the instruments," William added, who seemed not to notice her ragged appearance.

"Instruments? You mean there's more to it than just the singing?"

"Of course. Usually when I sing there's a violin accompanying me; there's a piano too."

Georgina's eyes widened. And that's what Danyell had wanted her to hear? "Are you not mad at me, for being here?"

"Mad?" He shook his head. "Of course not. Why should I? In fact, if you want me to, I can sing a few more songs."

"Could you?"

William nodded and pointed to a bench. "You just sit there, and then I'll sing a few more songs. But I can't stay too long, as I'll have to go home. My father is not too happy if I come home too late. It's not always safe on the streets, you know." He sighed. "I am afraid he's never very happy. But I suppose that's how fathers are. How about your father … is he happy with you?"

Georgina felt a sudden lump form in her throat, making it difficult to swallow. What little Uncle Doyle had told her about her father was not all that good. Apparently, both he and her mom had been killed by the police in a robbery gone wrong. She had no recollection of either of them since she'd been only three years old. It was then Uncle Doyle took her in and she came to live under his care.

Uncle Doyle always bragged about what a charitable deed it had been, caring for such a hopeless little wretch as she was. She should be eternally grateful that he had opened his heart for her.

She looked up and whispered, "I have no father, and no mother either."

William's face darkened with a tinge of sadness. "So sorry to hear that. So, you live ... by yourself?"

She shook her head and bit her lip. It was all she could do to keep from crying. "I live with Uncle Doyle."

She kept staring at her shoes and the thought occurred that William's father would surely be a lot better than Uncle Doyle. What was his father like? Rich probably. He seemed like a concerned man too, wanting William to be home on time. Would they have servants?

All of a sudden, the image of the chubby man with his fancy walking cane wormed its way back into Georgina's mind. What had the constable called him again? *Duffel, Buffel* ... No, Russell it was. And had he not told her that he had a son who was singing?

"Is your father perhaps Mister Russell?"

William's eyes widened. "Yes, how did you know?"

Georgina gave a nonchalant shrug. "I met him. Tonight, just outside of this church. He told me he had a son who would be singing."

William tilted his head and gave her an inquisitive stare. "He told you that?" He blinked a few times, as if trying to clear his head. Then he said in a sharper voice, "Were you with that fellow who tried to steal my father's cane?"

"Oh, have mercy on my soul. No, I was not." Georgina heard her own voice. It sounded silly. Desperate, really, and her original fears welled up again. Surely, William would now hate her. He would want her to leave, or worse, he'd call the constable on her after all.

"But you are wearing a boy's coat. My father said that a misfit tried to steal his cane and that he was with a girl in a boy's coat."

"It wasn't me," Georgina cried, almost on the verge of tears again. "Or, rather, it was, but I didn't come to steal that cane. I was coming to listen to the music with my friend Danyell. He was nice to me. He gave me this coat and a sausage."

"A sausage?"

"Yes," Georgina wailed. "I lost that too, and now I am wandering around, looking for a place to sleep, as I don't want to go back to Uncle Doyle. He just beats me and wants me to steal for him."

There. It was all out. And with her tale came a fresh wave of tears. She couldn't hold it back anymore. Now all was lost. Even William, who could sing so nicely and who had lifted her up for just a moment away from the horrible streets of Manchester with his music and had brought a touch of healing to her troubled soul, would hate her now. Her shoulders shook as she desperately tried to get control over her emotions, but that was easier said than done.

She felt his hand on her shoulder. Gentle, and light as a feather, but it almost brought as much comfort as his music had done. "Don't cry, Georgina," he said in a whisper. "Things will work out." He paused for a moment and then asked, "You said your friend is Danyell? What's his last name?"

Georgina looked up, and wiped a few tears from her cheek. "What do you mean?"

"His surname? He must have a surname?"

"I don't know," Georgina said while shrugging her shoulders. "Simmers or something. His father runs a grocery store. That's why he could give me the sausage."

"Simmons," William replied, and he sounded almost euphoric. "Danyell Simmons is my best friend. He often comes over to our house."

Georgina blinked her eyes. For a moment, everything was blurry. She swallowed hard, rubbed another the tear away and said, "He's been nice to me. Just about the only one."

William grinned. "That sounds like Danyell. Did he tell you he can play the violin? He's really good at it. And he is your friend?"

Georgina shook her head. "I don't know him so well. I just know him from meeting in the street now and then. We talk and he gives me things. That's all. I don't really have any friends." She sniffed and gave William a helpless stare. "I am not exactly the person people love to hang out with."

A painful silence followed. But then, and to Georgina's relief, William let out a chuckle and said, "Well, in my book you are a friend of Danyell, and a friend of Danyell is a friend of mine."

"You will not throw me out, then?"

He tilted his head. "Into the snow and the freezing cold? No way." He sat down on the pew next to her and shook his head. "Here's what I'll do ... I'll put you in the storage room for the night. It's warm there and I think I even know of a few blankets. That will keep you through the night. But tomorrow morning you have to be out of here before Mister Bartholomew comes in."

Mister Bartholomew. She'd heard that name, too. Wasn't that the vicar with that enormous grin? She pained her mind and then concluded he probably was. "Is he the man in charge?"

"Mister Bartholomew? Yes, he's the caretaker, the cleaner, the garbage man, and the gardener. He does just about everything there needs to be done in this section of the great cathedral."

"Is ... eh... he nice?"

William's face lit up with joy. "He's just about the nicest man I can think of. You don't have to worry about him."

"But you said he'll be angry if he finds me here."

William smacked his lips. "Not angry, no. But it's best not to give him a scare. After all, he only allows me in here by myself because he trusts I am not doing anything foolish."

"Such as putting a street girl into the storage room," Georgina replied with a little chuckle of her own. Her fears were gone, and she felt as if she could breathe again.

He nodded. "I suppose you could put it like that." He thought for a moment and then said, "Listen, I'll be practicing here tomorrow once more. I'll be all alone and will begin just after dark. Mister Bartholomew has given me a key. I'll bring you some food, and you can sleep here again. Then at least you have a place for tomorrow as well. Sound good?"

Sound good? Nothing could sound better. "Thank you," she said, barely audible while her fingers fumbled with the hem of her faded, broken dress. "But how can I be out of here on time if you lock the door?"

His face contorted in a frown. "Good point. I guess I'll have to wake you up before Mister Bartholomew comes in." He leaned forward and said in a whisper, "That will be our little secret and I'll bring you something to eat as well."

Georgina struggled to comprehend what was happening. This was most certainly one of the strangest days she'd ever had. One moment she was catapulted into sheer joy, only to be cast into utter darkness a moment later, after which another wave of sheer joy lifted her up again.

"William...", she said slowly, as if unsure whether to continue.

"What is it?"

"I-It's just that ... Well, I am a thief. I live on the streets. Why are you so nice to me?"

"I don't know," he stated with a serious look on his face. "You seem nice, and, as I said before, you are a friend of Danyell's."

"But I could steal all kinds of ornaments from the church."

"Sure, you could," he replied. "But you won't." His eyes now had a warm glow as they rested upon her. "Poverty is not synonymous with evil or wrongdoing. I know a few folks who are very rich, but you wouldn't want to live in the same house with them as they are ruled by selfishness and egotism. And ...," he paused for impact, "you liked the song that I just sang. That song was about God. If you were a wicked one, you would not have liked it."

So, that was it. That song was about God. Yes, the door to heaven was not in the big Cathedral. It was here in this simple, little side-building, and she had found it.

CHAPTER 5

❄

A door creaked, and the sound was immediately followed by heavy, approaching footsteps that left a strange, unwelcome echo that washed over the pastures. "Georgina ... Take care," a voice told her. "Someone is here who will send you back to the streets."

It was not an unfriendly voice, yet one that was clearly meant to disturb her peaceful rest. She tried not to hear the warning. Stretched out snugly on a sunlit lawn, where she enjoyed the warmth that washed over the wonderfully fragrant and flower-strewn fields, getting up was the last thing she wanted. She couldn't recall the last time she had felt so cozy and comfortable and she wasn't about to let anybody disturb her.

But the voice didn't want to be sent off. "Someone is coming, and they are going to send you back to the street."

"No, I don't want that," Georgina groaned, and turned around. "It's fine here. I don't want to go back to the street."

But the footsteps grew louder and stopped right at the door, and the voice kept pestering her. "Georgina, sit up!"

Gradually, the almost celestial presence of the fresh, warm grass disappeared and the musty smell of the storeroom where Georgina lay tucked away on and under a pair of sprawling blankets took over the lovely scent of the primrose, the grass, and the dainty spring bells near her head.

There was the rattling of a door handle, another creaking door which was followed by a loud, audible gasp. "Bless my soul … what on earth is going on here?"

It was then Georgina was abruptly jolted awake. All the unfamiliar sounds yanked her out of her cozy dream, and she sat up in alarm. She stared sleepily into the curious eyes of a man; a man she had seen before, but couldn't quite place right away.

He seemed utterly perplexed to see her. His bushy eyebrows were pulled up so high they stuck over his balding head as holly bushes at the edge of a hill. But his eyes were not cold and mean like the eyes of Uncle Doyle or those of Mister Paddy. Rather, they were the eyes of a man who had seen his share of trouble in the world, but who had learned that love is a much better answer to everything life offers than foolish hatred or stubborn bitterness.

He was old, but not ancient. A bit older than Uncle Doyle, and yet there was something boyish in his eyes as if seeing her reminded him of the time he was young himself.

And then, when he smiled, she knew who he was.

Mister Bartholomew.

It was the man who had welcomed all the spectators the night before with his silly little smile and his little bow. But now that she stared directly into his eyes, his smile didn't seem all that silly. Uncle Doyle's eyes never smiled, rather they would have been flashing with indignation in such a situation. But not these eyes. They seemed filled with something else. Was it concern or compassion? Georgina blinked her eyes, trying to comprehend. She just wasn't sure what to make of it. Could she even trust this friendliness? Maybe it was just the prelude to a harsh tongue-lashing, a sly and insincere way to get her to relax so that his anger would hit her that much harder. She had seen so little genuine care in her young life and been so devoid of human warmth that she remained tense and on edge, as if she were a mouse who had come face to face with the most horrible tomcat of the neighborhood.

Before she could answer, he spoke again. "Don't be afraid, little one. I understand it is cold outside. But how did you get in?"

She felt her face getting warm and looked around as if unexpected help could show up from the dark corners of the storage room. Where was William? He'd promised he would wake her up on time and open the door, so she had the time to get out before Mr. Bartholomew showed up. But he wasn't there.

"Don't be alarmed, child," Mr. Bartholomew spoke softly. "No harm will come to you."

Georgina sat up, her heart racing, and finally found her voice again. "I-I am sorry. I am not supposed to be here."

"That's rightly said," the man replied and, as a gesture of peace, he lifted both of his hands into the air. "But tell me, child ... how is it you got in?"

Georgina let out a cough and realized how stuffy the storage room actually was. She pushed her fears down. She needed to say something. But what should she say? If she told Mr. Bartholomew that William had let her in, he would scold William and maybe then he would not be able to practice there anymore. But how could she not tell the truth? William's kindness was the only explanation that made sense, and she preferred not to lie; not in this place where she had heard such heavenly music and where she could find the door to heaven. She heaved a long breath, and then, just as she was about to speak, she heard the door to the church open and close again, followed by approaching footsteps.

Mr. Bartholomew heard it too. His eyebrows went up again, and he took a step backwards to see who was coming.

"It's you," Georgina heard him say. "It's starting to make sense to me now."

William's resonant voice answered in a chirpy fashion as if everything was just as it was supposed to be, "Good morning, Mr. Bartholomew. How are you on this fine day?"

Georgina couldn't help but chuckle from within the storage room. All her tenseness left. Somehow, everything would work out. William had showed up.

"I am fine, young man," Mr. Bartholomew replied, "but I think you have some explaining to do. Look what I found in the storage room this morning." Georgina saw his face appear again and he ordered her to come out.

She got up from the floor and stepped outside. The light in the small side building of the great cathedral was blinding. The beauty of the day was evident in the way the sun illuminated the stained-glass windows in the front wall near the entrance. A beautiful display of a man who was lying in the arms of a weeping woman. She had not noticed its beauty before.

As soon as she saw William, she stepped in his direction and stood by his side.

"Well," Mr. Bartholomew spoke again, "what is going on here?"

"I- eh ... I can explain," William began, and he told the story of having met her the night before and about his desire to do something good. He ended his tale by saying something that for some reason seemed to make a lot of impression on Mr. Bartholomew: "If a brother or sister be naked, and destitute of daily food, and one of you say unto them, depart in peace, be ye warmed and filled; notwithstanding ye give them not those things which are needful to the body; what doth it profit?"

Mr. Bartholomew nodded, and Georgina dared to relax. Apparently, William had convinced him she was not a thief, and he would not call the police on her. In fact, the friendly expression still hadn't left his face. It made her feel somewhat warm, as if she was being accepted, something she was not used to. Still, it was best not to wear out her welcome and to go before more troubles would arrive, as they invariably always did. She bit the inside of her cheek and mumbled, "Eh ... thank you, William. But I'll be going now."

"Wait," Mr. Bartholomew said, and he made the stop sign with his hand. "Where are you going?"

"The street," Georgina whispered. Her mouth felt dry. "It's where I always go."

Mr. Bartholomew frowned. This time his bushy eyebrows came so low they almost touched his nose. "The street is no place for you."

Georgina gave a quick shrug and smacked her lips. "It's the only place I have."

"What about your uncle? Will he not be looking for you?"

"Probably."

"And that wicked fellow who tried to steal the cane last night? I understand he, too, is an unwanted acquaintance of yours."

"Mister Paddy?" A sense of anger arose, but it didn't last long. Mr. Bartholomew was right. They would be on the lookout for her. She had not considered her uncle's fury and while she had endured Mister Paddy for all these years, after his horrible stunt of the night before, she never wanted to see his ugly face again. She was done with her life of thievery and crime … if she could help it. But how could she survive without pilfering people's money, and where could she go?

Mister Bartholomew broke through her musing in soft tones. "Yes, I suppose that's who I meant."

Suddenly, Georgina felt weak, and her legs felt terribly wobbly. Or was it the floor that somehow was turning? She stumbled forward and grabbed hold of the pew, and big drops of sweat formed on her forehead.

William ran forward and helped her to sit down. "We'll find a solution," he said in encouraging tones. "Don't you worry."

But that was precisely what Georgina was doing. Last night, when she had decided to never go back to Uncle Doyle, life had seemed so full of promise. No clouds on the horizon in the daytime, and only starlit skies at night. But now, when the new day had arrived and reality stared her in the face, it all seemed so hopeless. A long silence followed; at least it seemed long to Georgina. She could only hear faint noises outside the church, noises that indicated life in Manchester had started again. A man was shouting his rude and impatient commands to his horse, and the Muffin-man was advertising his goods in loud, demanding tones somewhere far away. A muffin would be wonderful, but that too was just a fancy dream. She had no money for any food and it did not appear William had thought about her promised breakfast.

The picture of the river welled up. A dreadful thought, but she could always join the mud-larkers. By wading through the mud, you could get lucky and find stuff you could sell. She had always hated the idea, although Jimmy, a boy she didn't like, had told her he had found a silver coin once, and it had provided him with food for an entire month.

It was then that she felt Mr. Bartholomew's hand on her shoulder; fatherly, warm and caring. "Don't worry, child," he said in soft tones. "I've got an idea."

Both William and Georgina looked up in surprise.

"What is it?" William said.

Georgina said nothing. She kept as quiet as a mouse.

Mr. Bartholomew put on a serious face and narrowed his eyes again. "If I were to give you a job ...," he began, "... can I trust you not to steal anything of value here in the church?"

"A job?" Georgina's mouth sagged open. "W-What do you mean?"

"Work? Would you be willing to work for me?"

Georgina wasn't sure she heard right. "Of course, you can trust me not to steal. I don't want a life of mischief any longer, Mr. Bartholomew. Certainly, sure, I will be the best girl you ever had."

The caretaker nodded. It caused his shoulders to shake and Georgina suddenly realized the man was actually quite old already. "Promises are easily made, but most people just as easily break them," he stated in solemn tones. "However, something tells me I should trust you."

"Oh, yes you can, Mr. Bartholomew. Certainly. Sure." Georgina felt something bubbling up from deep within that she had never felt before. A glorious feeling; a mixture between excitement, gratitude and just plain joy. Someone trusted her. Nobody had ever trusted her before. And a job, a real job?

"What is it you want me to do, Mr. Bartholomew?" she asked, barely able to keep her voice steady.

"Clean the church. Dust the pews, mop the floor, that sort of thing. You'll be off the street; you can sleep in a normal bed and have two meals a day."

Two meals a day and a normal bed?

"Oh, Mr. Bartholomew, are you for real?"

The man flashed her one of his heartfelt smiles. "The Good Lord taught me long ago that His ways are ways of truth and kindness. I wouldn't dare tell a lie right here in the sanctuary."

Georgina turned to William and was tempted to run into his arms and hug him, but that would not be the right thing to do. Instead, while stumbling over her words, she said, "D-Did you hear that, William? I have a job."

His smile was almost as wide as Mr. Bartholomew's. "Will she stay in the storage room, Mr. Bartholomew?"

The old man shook his head. "That's a silly question, William. Although the Savior had nowhere to rest His head, I believe Mrs. Brooke has a spare room in our house."

"I - I can stay in y-your house?" Georgina wasn't sure she had heard him right.

"For as long as you behave, young girl," Mr. Bartholomew replied. "But first we need to get you some decent clothes, for the ragged clothes you wear right now are not fit for a servant girl of the Most High."

At those words a wave of coldness washed over Georgina. She pressed her lips together and began to fumble with her fingers.

"What is it?" Mr. Bartholomew asked.

Georgina hesitated. At last, she looked up into the old man's eyes and said, "I am not sure I can be a servant of the Most High. I have been a very bad girl, and what's more...," she stopped and looked down at the floor.

"Tell me," Mr. Bartholomew probed her in gentle tones. "You can tell me anything and everything."

Georgina fought to find the right words, but none would come. She looked up again and said, "I like the church ... It's beautiful. People say that here we can find the door to heaven..."

"That's about right," the old caretaker said. "That's why we have churches to begin with."

"But... But," Georgina mumbled, "I've been told that ... there is no God. That the rich people just invented God to keep poor people like me from being smart?"

She had said it, and a moment of deafening silence followed.

A scary, suffocating sensation crept up on her, and she could hear her own heart pounding. Oh, what if the old caretaker would now withdraw his kind and generous offer? How could he tolerate her in the house of God after what she had just said? And if God *did* exist, He surely would not want her either. They said God was holy, and she was as far removed from holiness as ... as ... Manchester was from London. To Georgina, that seemed awfully far.

Of course, if He didn't exist, there was no need to worry, but somehow, standing here, in the house of God and facing kind Mr. Bartholomew, she felt compelled to be completely honest. Lying and cheating seemed so awfully wicked. Why had she ever even done it? It felt so different here in the church. The silence, the beauty, and even the outside of the Cathedral ... everything seemed to draw her in, pull on her heartstrings. And then there was William's song. It had touched her in such an unusual and profound way.

People who believe in God are stupid, narrow-minded, and babyish. Don't fall for the lie. You yourself are the only real friend you'll ever have. Uncle Doyle's harsh, degrading and unbelieving words appeared in her mind, almost as if he were present and was shouting his version of the truth into her ear.

She shook her head, as if that would throw the fellow out. She no longer wanted him around. Maybe *he* was wrong, and he himself was falling for a grander deception that there was no God? Why should she even believe anything Uncle Doyle had taught her, since all he could think of was his own belly?

Then, to Georgina's surprise, Mr. Bartholomew broke out into a hearty laugh. His belly moved up and down and he laughed as if she had told him a most entertaining joke. "God doesn't exist?" he hiccupped. "Who said that?"

"My Uncle Doyle," Georgina replied, barely above a whisper.

Mr. Bartholomew wiped a tear away from his eye and while his shoulders were still shaking he said, "Well, my dear child, he is dead wrong. And if I may ask, is that the same uncle who is beating you and is forcing you to steal for him?"

Georgina just nodded. There was nothing else to say.

The old caretaker stepped forward and without hesitation put his arm around Georgina and pulled her close. "My dear child, you are afraid I will ask you to leave because you just told me you are not sure if God exists. Is that what's bothering you?"

How did he know?

Georgina looked up, still not quite sure what the man's next step would be, but when she saw the warmth in his eyes, her fears washed away. "Yes, Sir ... that's right."

"My child, you are welcome here. Mrs. Brooke will be thrilled to have you around." He paused for a moment and then said, "As far as you not believing in God, don't worry about it. There was a thief on the cross next to the Savior's and at first, he didn't believe either, but his story had a very happy end too."

Georgina had no idea what the man was talking about. She had never heard of a thief and a cross, but it sounded reassuring, and so she forced a timid smile on her face.

Mr. Bartholomew cast William a knowing look and mumbled something about how bad the world was getting. "And now," he said, "let's get you some new clothes. The ones you wear right now are awful."

CHAPTER 6

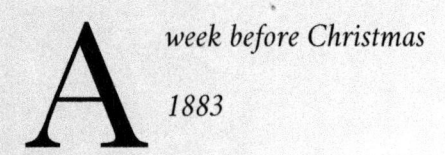

❄

A *week before Christmas 1883*

And so, Georgina's life changed overnight.

She could hardly believe her good fortune. Every day, upon opening her eyes in between her spotless, snowy linens and under a heavy, comfortable quilt displaying a heavenly band of singing angels, she would double-check if it wasn't a dream, by pinching herself.

No longer did she roam the streets of Manchester, trying to make a living by stealing and cheating for Uncle Doyle. All that had changed in a most incredible way, and she was determined not to do anything that would endanger her new way of life. She would be as good as the angels William had sung about, who were roaming the fields of glory and sailing the jasper seas. It struck her as odd that the moment she stepped away from Uncle Doyle and made a conscious decision to turn away from theft and crime, things had changed so drastically. Was that God's doing, or had she just fallen upon a stroke of good luck?

She had so many questions, but did not dare to ask Mr. Bartholomew. What if he decided she wasn't fit for a job in the sanctuary, since she was so full of doubts and confusion? It would be best to keep her mouth shut so she wouldn't look stupid or ignorant. A gentle voice whispered encouragement and told her she had nothing to fear. Mr. Bartholomew was very kind, and had assured her countless times she was safe. Yet, her long years on the streets and the harsh treatment by Uncle Doyle had left their marks. She was like a small, startled bird taken from her rusty, rickety cage, that had suddenly come face to face with a wonderful, wide world of blue skies and freedom where you could fly wherever you wanted without condemnation, punishment or fear. But to freely spread those wings and join other birds in a sky ballet of jubilation would have to wait a little.

To Georgina Mr. Bartholomew's wife, Mrs. Brooke whose name was Annabell, was the closest thing she'd imagined an angel to be. Angels would be like her. The dear woman had taken her in without question, and from the moment she arrived, treated her as if she was her own child. First, she'd given Georgina a bath. She placed a metal tub in front of the open fire, filled it with deliciously warm water, and gave her a good scrub. Halfway through the bath she plastered her with soap that smelled so wonderful, Georgina was certain the purifier must have come directly from the quarters of Queen Victoria herself.

"When was the last time you had a bath, child?" Mrs. Brooke asked. Georgina couldn't remember.

After she had washed her hair and rubbed her dry, she presented her with a new set of clothes. A wonderful blue dress with a white pinafore with little pockets that were edged with lace. Georgina gasped as she saw her new outfit.

Annabell raised her brows as she noticed Georgina's surprise. "I am sorry, they are not new," she mumbled in apologetic tones. "They are castoffs, but they seem nicer than what you were wearing. I hope you don't mind."

Was she kidding? Never had she had the chance to wear something so delicate and pretty. And these clothes were castoffs? Who'd throw away something so pretty? They smelled fresh too, like the lilies she had smelled once on a beautiful spring day in the park. No, these clothes made her feel as if she was a princess. At last, after she had made an elegant twirl for Mrs. Brooke and the dear woman had crowned her hair with a pretty, black bow of silk, she appeared to be a new creature.

Next came the food. That first day, she had pancakes. Real pancakes topped off with butter and cream. Georgina had a difficult time breathing as she sat down on a stately chair, which, according to Mrs. Brooke, was a castoff too. A member of their church had bought new furniture and given the old stuff to Mr. And Mrs. Brooke.

Again, Georgina had a hard time to relate. The chairs resembled thrones; the meal was suitable for royalty, and her new attire rendered her unrecognizable.

But, best of all was her new job.

Bartholomew Brooke showed her the work. Cleaning the stone floors, dusting off the pews, and many more such things. Just wonderful. What a breath of fresh air, as she no longer needed to manipulate and deceive men for a few coins. No longer did she need to run for her life, and Uncle Doyle was no longer present, except as an unpleasant phantom of the past. She couldn't help but chuckle as she imagined Uncle Doyle's rage now that she had run off. He would be furious. He would rant and rave, throw things around and then, as he always did, end up drinking himself into a stupor with the cheap liquor he always had money for.

She had been his primary source of income. Like Paddy, he was not a very good thief himself. He was too clumsy and totally unbelievable. His deception carried a pungent odor that would alert people a mile away, making it impossible for him to even come close enough to say hello. Maybe he would now have to go to the river and join the mud-larkers.

But she would not. Sleeping on a crackly floor under a dirty, faded blanket with holes that mice had chewed to take threads for their nests was no longer her experience. She now had an actual bed in clean surroundings in a loving, warm home.

Every night, the same sense of gratitude welled up; and every night she felt like uttering a prayer. But how and to whom? To God? But how could she be sure He would listen? And thus, she fell asleep every night, not quite knowing what to do with her longings.

William came to the church almost every day to practice his singing. At those moments, Georgina put down her work and listened in awe to the songs he sang. One afternoon, Danyell, who had brought his violin, joined him.

She sat spellbound as she listened to the sweet tones and the gorgeous singing.

Abide with me; fast falls the eventide;
The darkness deepens; Lord with me abide.
When other helpers fail and comforts flee,
Help of the helpless, O abide with me.

Help of the helpless? That sure sounded like the help she had received. Had she not been totally helpless? And right when things could not have been bleaker, help had come. Just like that. Oh, if it could be true that there truly was a God in the heavens. A deep yearning to yield to that most wonderful source rose in her heart and she determined to ask William about it as soon as she had a chance.

Right at that moment, the door to the hall opened and somebody entered.

Georgina sat in the pew somewhere in the middle and initially ignored the faint footsteps on the echoing church floor. But when William suddenly stopped in mid-sentence and Danyell stopped playing the violin as well, she turned to see who was coming.

It was a woman…

And she was beautiful too. She glided elegantly towards the pulpit, wearing a regal smile on her dainty face. Georgina marveled. Surely this woman was an emissary from Queen Victoria and came with a special message for William. Perhaps the Queen wanted William and Danyell to play and sing at a private party. That would make sense.

As she followed the woman with her eyes, suddenly she understood why Mrs. Brooke had said her marvelous new outfit was nothing but a castoff. While her clothes were nice, they were nothing compared to what this woman was wearing. In contrast to her, she appeared shabby and worn-out.

Georgina caught herself. This was not the way to think about the good fortune that had befallen her. She chided herself for even entertaining such an ungrateful thought and tried to push the thought away as she followed the woman with her eyes.

She was the kind of woman that made men stop on the street and cast her longing looks. Stealing from her class had always been Uncle Doyle's desire. Underneath the woman's blue mantle, she wore a matching blue velveteen frock with a lace collar and cuffs. A delicately woven shawl covered her slender neck, and a royal-looking bonnet covered her black hair that was carefully parted in the middle. She didn't acknowledge Georgina at all and instead floated onwards towards the pulpit, where she stopped in front of William and Danyell.

"Oh, my stars," she said in a honeyed tone of voice. "What are you doing here, William? I've been looking all over for you."

She knew William by name?

Georgina listened more closely. The woman talked to him as if he were her possession. That meant she was not a messenger girl from Queen Victoria at all. But why did she talk in such a sugar-coated voice? Georgina decided she did not like this woman. She knew that tone of voice all too well. It was the same wailing, sad and hypocritical outburst of neglect and undeserved suffering that she herself had used on countless occasions when she needed to relieve a stupid man of his money. This woman wanted something from William, and Georgina wasn't at all convinced William could see through her. She craned her neck so she wouldn't miss anything.

"Isadora," William greeted her. "I told you, I needed to practice my singing. You knew."

"Oh Honey-bear, I've been so bored at home. You know I really want you home at these hours."

Honey-bear?

"I am sorry, Isadora," William said, "but you know how important the singing is. I want to touch people's hearts with the Good News."

Isador shook her head. "It's time you are touching my heart, Honey-bear. I want you home with me and sit in the lounge on the couch so we can discuss important matters."

"Yes, like the weather," William replied, seemingly not impressed by the woman's suggestion. He cast Danyell a helpless glance, as if he was looking for moral support, but Danyell said nothing. Then his face brightened, and he looked straight at Georgina, as if a bright idea had come to him.

For a moment Georgina locked eyes with him and a strange, unfamiliar feeling of warmth shot through her body. He didn't just look at her, rather he looked into her. Nobody had ever looked at her like that, and she had never allowed it either. Not even Danyell. But William was welcome.

Before she could say or do anything, William jumped off the stage, took the woman gently by her shoulder and walked towards Georgina.

"Come, Isadora, I want to introduce you to someone. Maybe then you'll understand why my singing is important to me."

Georgina, not sure how to behave, got up, and wished she were not there at all. Her old, familiar fears resurfaced and she contemplated fleeing, yet that would display discourtesy; moreover, why escape when William was approaching, even though that strange lady was trailing behind?

"Georgina," William said as he stopped right in front of her, "let me introduce you to Isadora Cramps. She will be my … eh …," his voice trailed off, and he didn't finish his sentence.

"Fiancée," Isadora Cramps finished his sentence for him, as she gave Georgina an icy stare. "And who are you?"

William answered. "This is Georgina …" He wanted to add her surname, but apparently couldn't remember it.

Isadora Cramps did not give Georgina a second look. Instead, she turned to William again and said, "As I said, Honey-bear, we have things to discuss."

William rubbed the back of his neck, and instead of answering Isadora's question, he focused his attention again on Georgina. "Listen, Isadora, it's a remarkable story. Georgina was pretty much homeless; a girl on the street. But then, when she heard my singing, she compared it to the music of angels. And look how she looks now?"

Georgina wasn't at all sure she liked this conversation. While all he said was true, she did not like to be reminded of her life on the street; at least not in front of Isadora Cramps, who claimed she was going to be William's fiancée.

"She still bears the appearance of a commoner," Isadora said disdainfully, without even looking at Georgina. The magnificent blue dress and the white pinafore that Georgina had been so proud of were worthless. A wicked thought entered; an impulse to snatch the fancy ring that adorned Isadora's slender index finger away from her, run off, and sell it for a good price somewhere in the shady part of Manchester. She did not. Something told her to keep calm, and she was thankful she had the strength to listen to her inner voice of warning.

Fortunately, William did not share Isadora's sentiments. "You know I want to serve God, Isadora," he stated in a firm voice. "It's my prayer I can touch souls through my music, and Georgina is the perfect example it works."

"Oh, my silly Honey-bear," Isadora wailed, "you know that will not happen. Once we are married, you are going to take over the beer-brewery of my father. Oh, William, we will be so happy together."

William just sighed and began plucking at his shirt as if that was the source of all his discomfort. At last, he cleared his throat and said, "I'll be coming home soon, Isadora. You just get tea ready."

"That's what I have a maid for, William," she grumbled. "As I said, I want you home."

To Georgina, Isadora sounded sillier and more insincere by the second, but she said nothing. Anything she would say at this moment would be highly offensive to Isadora Cramps, and something told her it was best not to antagonize the woman.

At last, Isadora seemed to give in, as she nodded a goodbye to Danyell, cast William a last longing look and then got ready to leave. But just then she turned to Georgina, studied her for a moment, pulled her shoulders back, and stated with a gleam in her eye, "Georgina huh? I used to know a dog by that name. A wagon carrying horse manure ran her over." Her dark eyes bore into Georgina as if she were hoping for an angry reaction, but when Georgina said nothing, she just added with a slight grin, "And just so you know, there's a button missing on your dress."

Georgina's stomach roiled, and she felt heat rushing up to her face. Never before had she been wearing such lovely clothes, but Isadora made her truly feel as if she were back on the street.

"Isadora, please," William still tried, but the woman did not respond to his plea for kindness and friendship. Instead, she rolled her eyes, and without waiting for a response, she turned and walked off.

When the door closed behind her, William heaved a sigh of relief and he turned to Georgina. "Sorry about that," he mumbled. "I did not intend to cause you any distress."

"It's fine," Georgina said, and forced a weak little smile on her face. "But ... is ... is she really going to be your lady?"

William blushed and bit his lower lip. "It appears so," he said at last. "My father really wants me to."

"Your father?" Georgina arched her brows. "Why does he get to decide who you will marry?" Although her own life had been controlled by others in an oppressive environment, she found it odd that others would determine who you should marry. "Do you love her?"

"It's complicated." He let out an impatient groan, as if to show it really wasn't any of Georgina's business. "You wouldn't understand."

His voice carried a tinge of hardness, exposing an aspect of him she hadn't witnessed before. He turned to Danyell and said, "I need to go. Thanks for coming. See you tomorrow?"

Danyell nodded. "I'll be here, William."

Without saying another word, he walked off and left Danyell and Georgina in the deafening silence of the church.

Finally, upon hearing the forceful slam of the front door, Georgina mustered the courage to speak again. "What was that all about?"

"Isadora Cramps," Danyell replied. "She's his future wife."

"She reminds me of Paddy Slobcrude," Georgina said.

"Who?"

"Mister Paddy. Isadora Cramps has the same selfish look as Paddy. That's the dreadful fellow who tried to steal the walking cane from that man the other night."

"That was William's father," Danyell said.

"I know," she said, and a strange new truth dawned on her. Although William's life was vastly superior to hers, it transpired that every household had its own unique set of problems. "But does William love Isadora?"

"Don't know," he answered in a strained voice. "It's hardly my business, is it?"

Georgina narrowed her eyes. "It isn't, and it is. He's your best friend, isn't he? You should be concerned."

"Says the girl who lived an immoral life on the streets of Manchester," he fired back.

Georgina had not expected such a blow and for a moment, his words stunned her. Danyell seemed to realize he had gone too far, and held out both of his hands apologetically. "I am sorry," he wailed. "Forgive me, Georgina. I let my frustrations speak."

"Of course, I forgive you," she said, glad to see the Danyell again she knew. "Why are you frustrated?"

"To be honest, I don't like Isadora Cramps one bit. She's not my cup of tea, but her parents are extremely wealthy, and it appears William's father is determined to secure financial stability for his son. They run a very prosperous beer-brewery, but William wants to become a minister."

"A minister, what's that?"

Danyell pressed his lips together in a slight grimace. "He wants to live for God. Singing is his passion, and he wants to use his music to touch people's hearts."

Georgina instantly thought back on the night when she first heard William sing and how it had touched her heart in such a profound way. The words and the melody had enveloped her in a blanket of peace and security; as if everything in life would turn out all right. As if she did not need to fear, but she could just trust. A wonderful feeling it was and ever since that night a hunger, a desire had been created to know more.

"Do you believe in God, too?" she asked Danyell at last.

He tilted his head and seemed surprised. "Of course, I do. Don't you?"

Georgina felt a sensation of warmth flooding in. She would love to believe in God, but just didn't know how. "I don't know," she replied in a voice that was barely above a whisper. "I would like to, but nobody ever told me anything about Him."

Danyell looked at her for a moment, a peculiar smile playing around his lips. "In a few days, a Christmas play will be held here. The pastor will tell the story of Jesus' birth. William will sing, and I'll be among the musicians. It will be a lot nicer than on that evening when everything went wrong and they accused you of stealing the cane of William's father. You'll love it."

A Christmas play will be held? "I would love to see it," she said hesitantly, "but I doubt whether I can come." She looked at her dress and recalled the stinging words that Isadora Cramps had spoken. She was still a street girl and she'd always be one. "I - I am not sure if I am welcome."

"Not welcome?" Danyell's eyes flashed with anger. "Of course, you are. This is God's house and everyone is welcome here. On top of it, you are part of the Brooke's household now, so I don't see why you can't come."

"It would be lovely," Georgina whispered. Just the thought by itself was overwhelming, and a deep longing invaded her heart.

"Actually," Danyell said, "since you are now working in the church, I am sure Mr. Bartholomew will need you to make the arrangements. It's going to be lovely."

A real Christmas play with music and the true story about Jesus… For the moment, her distress about Isadora Cramps was gone. Life was good, and as far as she could see, it was only about to get better.

She would hear the Christmas story…

CHAPTER 7

❄

Danyell had been right. Mr. Bartholomew wanted Georgina to come. In fact, they had not even considered her not coming as Mr. Bartholomew needed her. "Listen, Georgina," he said, "you have an integral part to play."

"Me? Surely not, Mr. Bartholomew," Georgina mumbled, not comprehending what she could do for a Christmas play. "Danyell told me it's all about Christmas, and I know nothing about Christmas." And that was the truth. She had seen the Christmas frenzy on the streets of Manchester every year. Ladies and their husbands had their arms loaded with parcels, and most of the stores had their windows decorated with holly and other ornaments, but what the fuss was all about remained somewhat of a mystery. Uncle Doyle had done his share of lifting the veil by calling Christmas a lie. "It's a stupid feast for those who will not face up to reality," he told her once. "It's all about a baby that got born in some faraway land ... So what? Lots of babies get born every day, and lots of babies die every day too. No, it's a stupid feast." He snickered a bit and then added with a foul grin on his unshaven face, "And you know what?"

"What?"

"They claim the baby was born just like that."

"What do you mean?"

"Just what I said. They call it a miraculous birth. An illmaculate inception to use the right wording. But that's not possible. No baby gets born without a man and a woman doing the bear, if you get my drift."

Georgina was clueless. "I don't understand."

"Neither do I. Just take it from me, it's all rubbish. Fairy tales to escape reality. That's all Christmas is."

And that was about as much as she knew about Christmas, and since there was hardly any heat in their house, and no special food to celebrate anything, she had decided Uncle Doyle was probably right.

But now she wasn't so sure anymore.

"I need you to decorate the church," he replied. "I want the church to be spick and span. There should be lots of candles, and fitting Christmas decorations. Surely, you can help me with that, can't you?"

Georgina's eyes shone. "Oh, yes, Mr. Bartholomew, that sounds like fun."

"And fun it will be," Mr. Bartholomew said with a smile, "To me, the days leading up to the most wonderful feast of the year are almost as exciting as Christmas itself. And you'll learn about the meaning of Christmas soon enough. This service will put you in the right mood."

And so, she worked in the church with extra zeal. She scrubbed the stone floors as if she were polishing diamonds, she dusted the pews as if her life depended on it, and with Mr. Bartholomew's help she placed at least a hundred candles in strategic places around the sanctuary. It was going to be wonderful.

"You will sit here," Mr. Bartholomew said to her the afternoon before the service. He gestured to a pew situated directly in the center of the first row. "You will not miss a thing here. It's actually reserved for the wealthier folks in our community, but I think you fit right in and I want you to have a good view."

The wealthier folks in their community? Surely, she'd be better situated somewhere near the back, but Mr. Bartholomew would not hear of it. "Nonsense. You deserve to get a good look. Besides, you'll like the folks that will be sitting near you. They are good people, like William's father, and the Cramps. You don't know the Cramps, but they are a lovely bunch. They have a beautiful daughter too. She's a bit older than you are, but I am sure the two of you can become good friends. And …," he added in conspiratorial tones as if he was about to reveal a deep secret, "She's going to marry William one day."

She was going to sit near Isadora Cramps? That would spoil things a good deal. She realized there was not much she could do about it. At least Mr. Bartholomew and his wife would be nearby. That was a comfort. "Where will you sit, Mr. Bartholomew?"

"Me?" he said. "Nowhere. My wife and I are busy behind the scenes. We pick up enough of the Service to make it worth our while, but somebody has to take care of things. There'll be crumpets and roasted chestnuts after the Service, and somebody has to serve the drinks, and that somebody is not going to be you." Georgina heaved a long sigh. Crumpets were good, and so were roasted chestnuts. Isadora Cramps was bad. Maybe the good of a wonderful evening with the Christmas story and William's singing would outweigh having to sit near Isadora Cramps. It would all work out. She swallowed hard and said, "It's going to be lovely, Mr. Bartholomew."

He smiled and nodded. "Yes, child, lovely it will be."

❄

It was already dark when Mr. Bartholomew, his wife and Georgina made their way to the cathedral and the side-building where the Service would be held. A cold evening, it was. Temperatures had dropped considerably, but Georgina didn't mind. Danyell's winter coat kept her warm. What a wonderful gift that coat had been. When she followed Mr. Bartholomew outside, she saw to her great joy that it snowed. Tree branches were loaded with a fresh coat of holiness, and the happy, little flakes radiated with joy in the light coming from the street lamps. "Nothing is better than a Christmas with snow," Mr. Bartholomew said as he guided his wife and Georgina towards the church. "To me," he said, "nothing is better than people warmly tucked away inside their house near the hearth, while sharing the Good News of the birth of the Savior with a cup of hot chocolate milk in their hands, while outside God transforms the land into a wonderland of beauty and serenity. It will be that beautiful when our Savior has returned."

What that meant was a mystery to Georgina as well, but she did not want to ask. Mr. Bartholomew seemed so happy and cheerful that she didn't want to spoil any of his mood by asking questions that seemed out of line. And, of course, as far as the snow was concerned, he was right. All he said was true. Sitting in their home, now decorated with pine cones, holly and candles, while the flames in the fireplace warmed the very last fibers of her body was better than what she ever experienced before.

And yet, it confused her as well. What had she done to deserve all this? Uncle Doyle hated the snow and cursed every snowflake that came down. They had no warmth or luscious cups of hot chocolate milk, and talking about the birth of the savior was out of the question. But countless families lived just like she had then.

What made the difference?

"It's God, dear," Mrs. Brooke had said when she mentioned her doubts, while beaming her one of her gorgeous smiles with her radiantly shining blue eyes. "He loves you."

Did He really? But if Mrs. Brooke was right, and it was God, then why had he done it? What about those countless other poor folks living in their shacks near the place where she had grown up? People she had talked to, dressed in rags just like she had worn, who never had crumpets or roasted chestnuts, no warmth, and no future to look forward to?

She had mentioned it to William too and he answered her in similar terms as Mrs. Brooke. "Why do you think I don't want to take over the beer-brewery from Mister Cramps? I want to sing; touch people's hearts. I want to make a difference in this world ... I want to serve God."

It sounded lofty, and although she did not know what serving God even meant, seeing his zeal, and how his eyes lit up when he talked about it, made her realize that this was really William's dream. Marrying Isadora Cramps and working in the beer brewery would be a mistake. Of course, she said nothing to William about it. It was hardly her place.

When they arrived at the cathedral and made their way to the side-building, nobody was there yet.

They were early, as Mr. Bartholomew ought to be, being the caretaker. After they stamped the snow off their shoes, Mr. Bartholomew gave Georgina the job of lighting all the candles. Quite a job, but a wonderful one. "We are spreading the light, Georgina," he told her in his deep voice. "Christmas is the celebration of the light that has come into the world." With each candle she lit, the place became a bit warmer, but also a bit more mysterious. Georgina had loved the sanctuary from the first time she'd walked into it, but today it held a special beauty. When she was done with her job, and the sanctuary was bathed in a sea of flickering lights, she stared at it in awe.

Holiness. It was the only word she could think of to describe what she saw. Being here, in the sanctuary, seeing the lights and smelling the pine cones and holly that they had attached to the walls in various places, filled her with a peculiar joy, and she realized she wanted nothing better than to yield to such splendor. If this was what God was like, she wanted Him. She did not understand, but her longing for such purity was way stronger than her need to understand. For a moment, she closed her eyes and whispered a prayer, "God, if you are truly there, I too want to believe in you. Please tell me you are real. A warm feeling, such as she never had felt, rose from within. She felt like singing and suddenly, she understood why William wanted to sing, and why he wanted to serve God.

What could be better than to be a light-bearer; to light the lamps in people's hearts. To bring joy in places of sadness; to bring love where there was hatred and mischief...

"Georgina?"

Mr. Bartholomew's voice called to her, and Georgina looked up. "Yes, Sir?"

"The people are coming. Sit in the seat I showed you."

Georgina's heart jumped up, and her excitement knew no bounds. The evening was about to start and she hurried to the seat right on the front row.

Mr. Bartholomew had been right as people began to mill in. As before, Mr. Bartholomew stood at the entrance. He carried his grand smile again and did his best to make everyone feel welcome. Georgina was aware she carried a grand smile herself, but she couldn't get rid of it. It seemed to be glued onto her face, almost as if it was part of her.

William's father came in. A stately woman accompanied him; pretty with gentle eyes and a beautiful dress. Surely, that was William's mother. William's father leaned on his jewel-studded cane and scanned the pews. When he saw Georgina, he arched his brow, as if to say, "What are you doing here?"

Georgina didn't mind. Nothing could ruin this evening, and she had to admit, she even understood his reaction. The last time she had seen him, she had been wearing rags, and the constable had accused her of being a thief. If she'd been in his shoes, would she have reacted any differently?

He sat down in his pew, but made sure he did not come too close. His wife sat next to him on his other side. The pew next to her remained empty.

And then the Cramps came. At least Georgina assumed they were the Cramps, as she recognized Isadora. Haughty she looked, regal and cold. As soon as Isadora saw Georgina, she stopped her mother and whispered into her ear. Georgina could only imagine the message she passed on to her. Both women made sure they did not sit right next to her and left the place next to her open. Isadora's Pa would have to sit there. The man seemed clueless as to who she was and simply sat down, his face carrying a dignified smile. "Hello," he said, "I've never seen you before here. My name is George Cramps." He studied her for a moment and then added, "I am a beer-brewer. The best beer in Manchester carries my signature. And who are you?"

Normally, Georgina would have felt a dubious array of emotions. Nervousness, anger, even fear of being ridiculed or kicked out, but not tonight. She felt joy. Sitting here, in such a lovely place and about to hear about Christmas, was the best thing that had ever happened to her. God was here and had somehow heard her brief prayer. Danyell was right. What was it again he had said? *"This is God's house and everyone is welcome here."* If this was truly God's place and she was welcome, then there was nothing to worry about. So instead of lowering her eyes in shame and uncertain embarrassment, or looking up at him in defiance while she contemplated the best way to relieve him of a few silver coins, she looked straight at him and said with conviction, "I am Georgina and I help Mr. Bartholomew in the sanctuary."

Isadora's father raised his brow and mumbled, "Is that so?" It was then that his wife pulled at his arm and ordered him to not speak to her any longer.

Georgina didn't mind. While she had been so nervous about meeting the Cramps, their proud, condescending attitude couldn't bother her tonight. It was as if everything inside her was singing and nothing could disturb her happiness.

She turned to look around to see if she could spot Danyell or William, but the lights were too dim and also, they would likely be back stage, preparing for whatever it was they would do tonight. There was a pleasant buzz. Everyone was talking, and it was noisy and finally, when Mr. Bartholomew closed the church doors and everyone had found a place, a tall, slender man with a beard climbed onto the stage and motioned for silence with his arms.

Someone in the pew behind Georgina whispered, "Quiet, Pastor Plundell is going to speak."

"So, he is the pastor." Georgina eyed him with renewed interest.

He donned a frock coat that was cropped, featuring a hemline that ended at the midway point of his thigh. His straight trousers had no pleats around the waist, but none of that was of any importance to Georgina. What struck her was his general demeanor. His eyes radiated with a tranquil conviction, much like she had witnessed in William. It gave him an appearance as if he was unacquainted with wickedness and deceit. Very intriguing. Georgina sat up straight and pricked up her ears.

He welcomed everyone, made some general statements, and then explained what would happen at the service. When he was done, he invited everyone to join him in the singing of a hymn. From somewhere in the back the majestic tones of an organ arose and the whole congregation broke into singing as one. Everyone, except Georgina. She had no idea what to sing, but it sounded wonderful. She closed her eyes and let the singing wash over her. At one point, she opened them again and studied the surrounding people. They were all singing. Isadora was too. She sang at the top of her lungs. Her mouth, intricately and beautifully lined, moved rhythmically up and down and, Georgina had to admit, she had an absolutely lovely voice.

. . .

"God loved the world of sinners lost and ruined by the fall; Salvation full, at highest cost, He offers free to all."

Georgina wasn't sure what it all meant, but it was obvious they were singing about something that was just as holy as everything else here in the church.

Suddenly, there was a change in the atmosphere. It was Isadora. The woman had caught Georgina's stare. The whole church was just bellowing out: *"Love brings the glorious fullness in,"* but the lyrics froze on Isadora's lips. Her sanctimonious expression disappeared even faster than Paddy Slobcrude had in his run to safety on the day the mob had caught him trying to steal the jewel-studded cane.

Georgina tried smiling at her. Showing Isadora that she meant well would help. After all, the woman had a beautiful voice, and tonight she could take on the world and that included Isadora Cramps.

Sadly, Isadora could not. Georgina's efforts were in vain. Isadora stopped singing and stared staunchly ahead without giving Georgina another look. Georgina noticed the clenching of her jaws. Why was she like that? She had done nothing to hurt Isadora.

Then again, maybe it was understandable. It would be hard for a woman like Isadora to accept her just like that. She had come in from the street and couldn't even properly read or write. Her education had been centered on fraud and deceit and then there was William. Surely, Isadora had noticed how fond she was of William.

If it were possible Georgina would go over to Isadora right at this moment, place her hand on her shoulder, and say: "I understand, Isadora, and you are right. I am a misfit. I don't belong here, and don't worry, I will never be in William's mind. How could I?"

Of course, she could not do that. Nobody would understand. More likely, Isadora's mother would interpret her attempt at kindness as a violent attack on her daughter and call in the help of the ushers to relieve them of this hornswoggler.

She tried to concentrate again on the Service. The hymn was over, and Pastor Plundell announced in a booming voice that the main events of the evening could fully begin. After these words, he stepped off the stage and disappeared behind the curtain.

A holy hush settled on the church, and everyone waited in anticipation for the things to come.

CHAPTER 8

❄

Suddenly, beautiful, almost plaintive tones filled the church, echoing off the high ceilings. Georgina stretched her neck to see where the sound was coming from. The melody seemed to reverberate from around the pulpit, even though no one was standing there yet. She understood the violinist was standing out of sight behind a red, velvety curtain. It came to her in a flash. It was Danyell who was playing. They had asked him to start the evening, and what a start it was. The melody permeated the air and covered everything and everybody in the church like a mighty wave that rolled in from the ocean, refreshing and invigorating the hearers. It filled every crack on the dry sandy beach of Georgina's heart. How strange that a world so filled with music and beauty had never reached her before.

Music was another language. It was a language William understood and spoke. Music talked of things that could not be put into words and had the power to lift you out of yourself.

She closed her eyes and let the melody take her on its celestial wings to realms she had never visited. Then there was a calm. The violin stopped for a moment. Only for a moment, but when the music came back, this time a deep, rich voice joined in. Or rather, the violin accompanied the singing.

She opened her eyes again and saw that William had come onto the stage and he was the one singing, warm and melodious. It was not the song he had sung that first night. She had never heard this melody, but it was as beautiful as all the other songs she had heard from him.

She understood from some whispers that encircled her he was singing a Christmas carol. How was it she never had caught on to the beauty of Christmas? It seemed she was not the only one who liked the singing, as a reverential stillness descended on the church. Surely, Isadora Cramps would be touched as well. She momentarily allowed herself to steal another glance at the woman. She appeared as a fish out of water. While most people hungrily feasted on the beauty that William and Danyell served them, Isadora Clamps seemed not to be impressed. She still looked staunchly ahead. Not a muscle in her beautiful face moved.

Georgina forced herself back to the beauty of the singing, not wanting any unpleasant vibes from Isadora to spoil the music. Not a difficult task. If Isadora wanted to have the woefuls she could have them, but Georgina was not about to let her mood be spoiled. Her heart fluttered as she immersed herself once more in the music. As she listened, she realized that all her life a heavy black curtain had been placed over her heart. A dark, smothering blanket that prevented any light from trickling in. But now, with each word of the Christmas carol and each tone of Danyell's violin, the covering was ripped off, bit by bit, sentence by sentence.

> *But with the woes of sin and strife*
> *The world has suffered long;*
> *Beneath the angel-strain have rolled*
> *Two thousand years of wrong;*
> *And man, at war with man, hears not*
> *The love-song which they bring; –*
> *Oh hush the noise, ye men of strife,*
> *And hear the angels sing!*

Oh, she heard the angels sing all right.

The song transported her to a sphere of glory where everything was good and where strife ceased to exist. If this was Christmas, then she wanted every bit of it.

At last, the song was over.

She couldn't resist glancing at Isadora. There was no change. She still carried her scowl.

Pastor Plundell came back on and began talking about shepherds in the field. He mentioned angels singing in the heavens, and the birth of a baby in a manger; a baby who was to become the Savior of the world. He finished by saying, "And they called the child Jesus, for he would save the people from their sins."

The curtain that had kept Georgina's heart in the dark for so long was fully drawn. Atop a mysterious, yet marvelous mountain of victory, she stood gazing not only at the winding road she had traveled but also at an incomprehensible future of hope and bliss stretching for miles ahead.

Her mind could not fathom the bliss she felt; she could not explain it in sensible words, but one truth stood out; one certainty emerged like a stable rock in a tumultuous sea: God was real and it was this knowledge she had unknowingly been longing for all her life. Everything Uncle Doyle had said about God, the Bible, prayer, and even Christmas had been false. In fact, everything about Uncle Doyle was false, and she would never again carry the yoke of his oppressive service. She was free. Truly free.

More hymns came. More wonderful melodies from Danyell's violin, and more announcements were made by Pastor Plundell, but Georgina could no longer fully concentrate. She felt as if an invisible hand carried her through the church and words of affection and healing were whispered to her wounded heart.

And then the Service was over.

Pastor Plundell still mumbled something about roasted chestnuts and hot tea, and everyone got up. To her surprise, Georgina noticed her cheeks were wet. She had not even realized she had been crying. People started talking, some laughed loudly; one lady gave a shriek and accused someone of stepping on her toe, and a few children started running wildly through the church, relieved and happy the service was over. The Cramps left too. They were careful to move away from Georgina so they did not need to pass near her. Isadora did not look at her. It didn't matter. Nothing mattered. To Georgina, this had been by far the best night of her life. She had looked forward to the crumpets and the roasted chestnuts, but not anymore. She just wanted to sit still in silence and did not want the evening to stop. And so, she stayed put in her seat, while the noise and tumult of the other spectators moved away to the crumpets and chestnuts.

"Did you like it?" A voice asked her from behind.

She turned and looked into the shiny eyes of William. "D-D-I like it?" Georgina stammered. "I had the best evening of my life. And you know what?"

"What?"

"I believe in God. Now I understand why you want to sing for Him. Oh, William," she said, and in her sincere excitement she just grabbed his hand and squeezed it. "And I want to live for Him too. Now I understand you."

William was visibly shaken, so much so that he did not even pull his hand away. For a moment, he just stared at her in stunned silence. Then he said, "I am so very glad, Georgina. Few people understand this. It's like you have found the pearl of great price. I too have found it. It's why I sing."

"And it's so beautiful, William," Georgina said, and she really meant it. "I wish it could always be like this."

"But it can," William said. "It says in the Good Book, "All the days of the oppressed are wretched, but the cheerful heart has a continual feast.""

"It says that?" The picture of Uncle Doyle and Mister Paddy's wretched lives appeared, and how much better to have a cheerful heart. How wonderful would it be if she could read that book for herself. She looked up and a lump formed in her throat. "I don't know the Good Book. In fact, I can't even read."

A genuine smile appeared on William's face. "I'll teach you. It's not too difficult. Then you can read the entire story for yourself."

"You mean it?" Georgina blinked. How much more beautiful could this evening become? "You mean I can learn how to read the Christmas story for myself?"

"Yes indeed, the whole story."

"And I can read about pearls of great price?" Oh, how lovely had it sounded when William had said it.

"You can even read about the Pearly Gates."

Georgina wanted to jump up and down and dance, if only she knew how to do it. Instead, she turned to William and their eyes locked. She wanted to say a thousand things, but nothing came. William looked back. His eyes were so warm, so inviting and so trustworthy, as if they led to a pool of delicious warm water in which she could swim and wash herself from all her dark past.

Then he did the unthinkable. Instead of withdrawing his hand, which was still clasped by Georgina, he put his other hand over Georgina's and held her tight. It felt natural. Normal, as if it were meant to be. He curled his lip and said, "We will start tomorrow with our first lesson. We'll have a wonderful time."

"What's going on here?" A sharp, harsh female voice sounded through the empty church and cut through Georgina's heart. Abrupt, brisk footsteps reverberated across the stone floor. The woman, in an excited, high-pitched voice, uttered a strange expression that Georgina had never even heard on the street before. The meaning, however, was crystal clear and left nothing to the imagination. Somebody was furious.

It could only be ... Isadora Cramps.

Georgina pulled her hand away and turned to look. She had been right. It was Isadora. Beautiful Isadora, with eyes that could kill and were as cold as the River Irk when it was frozen over. She was clenching a half-eaten crumpet in her fist. Tiny morsels of the delicacy were still plastered around her red lips. William was blushing and got up, facing the approaching storm.

The warmth and the joy of the moment were gone. A wave of terror and uncertainty washed over Georgina's heart, much like on that night when they accused her of being in cahoots with Paddy Slobcrude when he ran off with the stolen cane. The so familiar, chilly feeling of loneliness that had ruled her heart for so long, stuck up its ugly nose once again. What had she been thinking? She had always been an outcast, and she would always be. How could she have been so foolish, so careless, as to hook up with William like that, even holding hands? Surely, this would mean the end of her stay at Mr. Bartholomew's place.

Isadora was in a different class. She was the woman about to be engaged to William. Her father was an important man in Manchester; a beer brewer. No, this time she had really messed up. The glass-stained windows in front of the church spun, and while her heart skipped a beat, her mouth filled with a choking sense of dryness.

"I am with you. Fear not. You are in My hands."

A still, small voice, but yet clear and reassuring, spoke to her heart. Was that the voice of God? If that were true, she could have faith in it and grasp onto the words as if they were a life-buoy. Then she did not need to be afraid. She had met God. She was in His hands.

Her dizziness left. The glass-stained windows stopped their sickening swaying. Her heartbeat returned to normal, and the dryness in her throat disappeared. Without waiting for William to defend himself, she spoke up with a boldness she knew not she possessed, and said, "I know what it looks like, Isadora, but I can explain. This evening has been so special that in my clumsy excitement, I grabbed hold of William's hand. There's no reason for you to worry. There's nothing going on between the two of us. Certain and sure. William is yours and I apologize."

She wasn't sure what to expect from Isadora, but she hoped her attempt at humility would be sufficient to restore peace in the woman's troubled mind.

It was not to be. The anger that rolled out over Isadora's red lips came as an unexpected blow. She shifted her gaze to Georgina and stared at her with eyes teeming with loathing so potent that even Uncle Doyle's explosive tantrums were mild in comparison. "You are nothing but an undesirable varmint. A no-good thief from the streets, a leech that seeks to prey on the unsuspecting good people of society to benefit your own miserable cause. I want you out of my life, and out of this church, or else ..." Seething with rage, she squeezed the last bit of her crumpet to a pulp in her angry, sweaty hands and yelled, "Do you understand?"

"Please, Isadora ..." William stepped in. He assumed a remorseful pose by raising his hands and added, "Don't get all uptight and listen to what she has to say. She's absolutely right. There's absolutely nothing going on between us. She just found faith in God. We should rejoice like the angels in heaven."

Isadora turned to him with a scowl. "Rejoice like the angels in heaven? How can I rejoice when I see my future husband squeezing the hands of a ratbag, a dying duck in a thunderstorm? Rather, I believe the angels in heaven have their eyes filled with tears."

"Not so," William lamented. "You take everything the wrong way, Isadora."

"Do I?" Isadora cried out in a loud voice. "Then tell me I am wrong. Tell me you despise this hedge-creeper, this hornswoggler.

Normally, such terrible insults would have infuriated Georgina, but strangely enough, she could not feel anger. She stared at the woman with her bitter rant and felt an unfamiliar ache; almost a yearning to step forward and put her arms around Isadora and tell her that everything would work out. It was a nearly incomprehensible urge, but she decided against it. It would likely only intensify Isadora's fury.

William did not seem to share Georgina's sentiments of compassion. She saw his face redden. "You have no right to call Georgina such names," he hissed. "I demand an apology."

Isadora blinked her eyes and, for a moment, stared at him in deep bewilderment. At last, she mumbled, "Deceived ... The devil in that girl has deceived you."

William didn't know what to say. He threw his arms up in despair, shook his head, and let out a long, frustrated sigh. Georgina wished she was invisible. Things had been so wonderful, but all of a sudden, it was as if the ground had opened and dark thoughts crawled out like ugly, poisonous spiders on a mission to take away her frail, newfound joy.

But then it looked like Isadora's anger was over. The raging storm that had made her stomp her feet and prompted her to say things that should never have come out of the mouth of such a sophisticated woman had subsided. Her demeanor changed. She put on a smile and she grabbed William's hands. "Come, Honey-bear, let's leave. Let's go home and forget tonight. We should not fight."

"I am not fighting," William insisted. "I just want you to —,"

"— Please?" she insisted in a pouty, little voice. "Let's go to my house. We'll have a glass of Sherry and forget this whole terrible incident."

At that moment, the door to the sanctuary opened, and Isadora's father appeared. "Isadora, our carriage is ready," he called out. "We are waiting for you."

When he saw William, a sanctimonious smile slipped across his face and as he walked in their direction, he said kindly, "Are you coming too, William? There are actually some things I would like to discuss with you."

William was conflicted and of two minds. He looked from Georgina to Isadora and back to Georgina. Then he nodded and asked, "What things, Mister Cramps?"

"I have some important decisions to make about the brewery. As you know, beer is the life stream of my blood, and since it will be yours as well, I would like to discuss some important changes."

Georgina could see William cringe, but she knew she could say nothing. None of this was any of her business.

At last, and to Isadora's relief, William made up his mind and agreed to go with the Cramps. But before he walked off, he still turned to Georgina, and with his eyes moist and warm he said, "This was a memorable evening, Georgina. And I meant what I said about teaching you to read and write. We'll work it out."

Georgina could see Isadora narrowing her eyes. *Please, dear God, not another outburst of anger.*

She made herself as small as possible and while she wanted to run up to William and thank him for being so kind and considerate, (not something she would do at this moment in a thousand years) she got up and whispered, "Thank you, William, but I will have to decline. I don't think we should see each other again. Isadora is right. She is your fiancée and I should have been more considerate. I am sorry."

"But ... but ...," William argued, "You did nothing —,"

"— That's the first sensible thing I've heard from this girl," Isadora gloated. "Now let's go home."

Georgina steeled herself and made her way out of the church. She could feel Isadora's triumphant spirit in passing. As she opened and closed the door to the sanctuary, she heaved a sigh of relief. The crumpets and roasted chestnuts would have to be eaten by other folks. She wanted to be alone, out on the deserted Manchester streets. Her mind was in turmoil and her heart deeply stirred. And yet, she was no longer alone. Somehow, that gnawing, sickening sense of misery, of not being worth her place in this world, and of being destined to live life without a friend was no longer present. Whatever was going to happen, she had a friend in God. He had spoken to her heart that she did not need to be afraid because He was with her. And, if someone as big as God was with her, then who or what could be against her?

What a lovely thought it was. As she stepped into the snow and pulled the coat, she had gotten from Danyell tight around her shoulders, she almost felt like singing. Despite the encounter she'd had with Isadora, this was still the best night of her life.

As she turned the corner, she hummed the words of the hymn she had heard that evening.

Oh hush the noise, ye men of strife,
And hear the angels sing!

CHAPTER 9

Georgina slept soundly that night. When she awoke, to her delight, the joy of her experiences of the night before still lingered in her heart. However, something else also persisted there, which was somewhat more unsettling. While she had felt such peace about the harrowing encounter with Isadora the night before, this morning, the woman's ugly insults stared her right in the face. They cast a shadow over the peace she felt with God as a storm cloud that obliterated the sun. While in the church, and later, when walking alone through the deserted streets of Manchester, she had derived such comfort and courage from the thought that God was watching over her. But now reality kicked in. Isadora had a powerful father who could move people around at his command, and she had greatly offended his daughter. She had also heard that beautiful and mysterious voice that assured her she did not need to worry and fear. But that had been last night. Would that count for today, too? What if she had imagined the whole thing and before this day was over, she would be back on the street?

But she had *not* imagined it. God would help her. He would take care of her ... *Would He?*

Thus, she was tossed back and forth between the desire to sing and thank God, and the urge to crawl back in a hole like a frightened mouse. Would Mrs. Brooke catch her confusion when she showed up for breakfast?

She would soon know.

"Good morning, Georgina," Mrs. Brooke said in cheerful tones. She was stirring the bacon on the stove next to a steaming cup of hot tea. "How did you like the Service last night?"

Georgina pulled out a kitchen chair and sat down. "It was absolutely wonderful, Mrs. Brooke."

"I knew you would like it," Mrs. Brooke said as she took the skillet off the fire and scooped part of the bacon on a plate before Georgina, right next to a neat pile of scrambled eggs and fried potatoes. "I made the bacon extra crisp, just the way you like it."

Right when Georgina thought her bewilderment went unnoticed, Mrs. Brooke caught on. While sipping her tea, she tilted her head and a curious look appeared on her wrinkled face. "Oh, my stars," she exclaimed. "Do you mean it? I can't tell from your expression and it confuses me. Did you perchance catch a fleeting sight of the Pearly Gates last night, or did you, by chance, cast a glance into the other world? What's going on?" Mrs. Brooke pulled out a chair and while placing her steaming cup of tea on the table, she sat down, demanding the full scope.

"Well ...," Georgina began hesitatingly, "William's singing was absolutely superb. It lifted me away from this mundane world and showed me there's more to life than just making it to the end of another day. Certain sure." Her eyes shone again as she recalled her experience.

"I see," Mrs. Brooke said. "That's the pearly gate part..."

A feeling of peace came. Talking to Mrs. Brooke was so easy. "I am not sure what you mean by the Pearly Gates, but yes, it feels like I've seen them. You know, I think I believe in God now."

Mrs. Brooke smiled. Her smile was almost as grand as her husband's. "Well, that's most wonderful, dear. I have prayed for you."

"Have you?" Georgina looked up into Mrs. Brooke's kind eyes, surprise etched in her eyes. "I don't think anybody ever did that for me."

"We both did; my husband and I. You are a precious child, Georgina. A child of the King."

A child of the King? How wonderful did Mrs. Brooke make it sound. It reminded her of the words of the hymn William had sung. She wanted to put her arms around the dear old woman, and just hide in the shelter of her bosom. Warm, safe, and secure. It almost felt as if Mrs. Brooke was her mother; a mother she'd never had and who would always be there to speak words of comfort and encouragement. Leaning like that to Mrs. Brooke, however, seemed like an awfully awkward thing to do. Instead, she stared at her bacon and aimlessly poked with her fork in an especially crisp part.

"And now the other part," Mrs. Brooke asked in gentle tones. "What's bothering you? It seems you had such a wonderful experience; what could have spoiled it?"

The face of Isadora Cramps wormed its way back into the forefront of her mind.

Isadora had not called her a child of the King. She had called her different names and it hurt, the worst being she was not altogether wrong. While she didn't even know the meaning of some things Isadora had called her, she probably was all those things. Hadn't she been a cheat, a fraud, and a liar? Thinking of Isadora and her rich, powerful father snuffed out her flame of hope. It was as if somebody had cast a smelly old wet blanket over her. She felt Mrs. Brooke's eyes boring into her and her ears getting red. How could she explain all this?

She swallowed hard and then blurted out, "I - I - am not sure if I may stay here, I mean with you and Mr.

Bartholomew. I've been so happy here, and I love to help in the church, but ..." Her voice trailed off.

"But what?" Mrs. Brooke asked while she leaned forward and narrowed her eyes into tiny slits. "What nonsense is this, my child? We are most happy to have you."

"I think I offended Isadora Cramps."

Mrs. Brooke said nothing. She just took in what Georgina had said. At last, she gave a small nod and said, "You mean you offended William's fiancée?"

Georgina lowered her eyes and gave Mrs. Brooke a small nod in acknowledgment. "Well," Mrs. Brooke said, "not much is needed to offend her. I never understood what William sees in her and if you ask me, she's as high and mighty as the proud ermine who is mostly concerned with not soiling her precious fur."

Georgina looked up, surprised at the words of the caretaker's wife. She didn't like Isadora Cramps? A devious smirk danced around the older woman's mouth as she quipped, "But don't tell anyone I said this. Let it be our little secret. But what happened?"

"William's music touched me so much. In the end, when the church was empty, he walked up to me and asked me what I thought of the evening ..., Oh, Mrs. Bartholomew, it was so lovely, and for the first time ever, heaven seemed real. But then ...," she hesitated.

"Then what?"

"Then ... eh ... I grabbed his hand, and he grabbed mine. She saw us and was furious."

"I see. And now you are afraid she's going to use her father's power to get you back on the street?"

A tear, unexpectedly, rolled out. Georgina nodded. "She said that if she would ever see me back in church, she'd do something. Her father seems awfully powerful."

"That he is," Mrs. Brooke agreed, "but he's not nearly as powerful as the God you found." She stroked Georgina's hair and added, "Fear is a terrible thing, Georgina. It's almost our biggest enemy, but as they say, soup is never eaten as hot as it is cooked. This is where faith comes in."

She wanted to say more, but just then there was a loud, insistent knock on the door. Mrs. Brooke looked up. "Who could that be so early?" She got up from her seat and walked towards the front door while mumbling something about the world always being in a hurry.

Georgina felt a lot calmer. The fact that Mrs. Brooke didn't seem to be too keen on Isadora was a great comfort, and that, coupled with her serene demeanor of faith brought peace. How wonderful if you could just say what you really felt without having to fear the consequences.

Bacon and eggs! Crumpets ... fruit!

Suddenly, her eyes were drawn to the delicious breakfast Mrs. Brooke had served her, and she realized how hungry she was.

Mrs. Brooke returned. "Eh ... Georgina?"

She just had taken her first bite and couldn't answer immediately. Instead, she turned, and looked into the smiling eyes of William. "Good morning, Georgina," he said. "I came to discuss when we can have our first lesson."

Georgina felt the heat in her cheeks rising. She swallowed her bite and mumbled, "William ... what are you doing here?" She looked in bewilderment at Mrs. Brooke, but the woman just gave her a knowing little smile and said she needed to take care of laundry. After these words she withdrew herself. Georgina could hear her walking about in the pantry. She had to confront William alone.

He sat down at the same place Mrs. Brooke had sat earlier. "Well," he said, "When can we start? Do you have a break in your work at the church?"

While it felt wonderful to have William around, it also felt extremely uncomfortable. She bit the inside of her cheek, threw her fork down, and said, "William, I told you I can't see you anymore. Isadora will be enraged and she threatened me with ... with ..."

"With what?" William replied calmly. "Dogs that growl and bark the most are usually cowards and are the most scared."

"But her father is a powerful man. He can have me removed from here. Then I'll be back on the street."

William shook his head. "That will not happen. I am actually glad about what happened last night."

"Glad?" *How could he be glad?*

He grinned and then crossed his arms while leaning back in his chair. "You seem surprised?"

"I am. How can you be happy after having an argument with the woman you love?"

"That's the point. I realize more than ever that I don't love Isadora. I do not want to be engaged to her, and I do not want to marry her. I'll tell her later today. I will break off the engagement."

"What?" Georgina wasn't sure she heard right. "But you are going to be rich by marrying her. You will inherit the Black Swan Ale Brewery. I've heard that the Cramps sell their beer even on the continent; in Holland and Belgium, and even as far as in France. Not marrying her would be a mistake."

"But I don't *love* Isadora … And I like Black Swan beer even less. Did you ever taste it? If you ask me it tastes like unwashed socks."

Georgina burst out laughing, which broke the tension she felt rising. But when the laughter was over, she asked in serious tones, "Is it my fault? I am so sorry I held your hand last night. I should have known better."

A wide smile appeared. He uncrossed his arms and shook his head. "No, Georgina, it has absolutely nothing to do with you; or at least I should say, it is not your fault."

He paused to reflect and then said with a faraway look, "I never liked her, but there has been so much pressure from both my father and the Cramps alike. But how can you compel someone to marry against their wishes? It just isn't right. But you holding my hand yesterday made me realize that. Seeing how happy you were with the singing, how it touched you so deeply, and how it helped you to see God in a new light, opened my eyes and has given me the courage to follow the way I feel God is leading me. It made me realize I cannot ever give up my dream of singing for God. More than ever, I want to give Him my talents in that way."

"But she'll be mad!"

William scowled. "That may be true. But then again, when is she not mad? I understand that to you, having lived in dire poverty, it may seem unthinkable that I will turn down the offer of running a beer brewery, but believe me, I don't really care for money all that much."

"You don't?"

"No, I don't. Don't forget, I wasn't raised in poverty either. Money is not all that it is made out to be." He lifted a finger in the air and said, "That's why I want you to learn to read. There are some wonderful passages in the Bible about earthly riches and how useless money is, and it would be most wonderful if you could read them for yourself."

Georgina touched her temple and closed her eyes, hardly believing what she just heard.

"So," William asked, "when will we start?"

"You are serious, aren't you?"

"Dead serious. Certain sure."

Georgina couldn't suppress a smile. This was such wonderful news. "Can I ask Mr. Bartholomew? After all, he is my boss."

"Of course," William said, "but there's more."

"More?"

William pressed his lips together while a suspicious looking grin flashed over his face. "You like my singing, right?"

"Oh, William, I absolutely love it."

"Well ...," he paused for effect, "... how about it if you ..." He raised his finger again, "... will sing with me?"

Georgina's hand flew to her chest, and she stared at William as in a daze. "Me singing with you?" she stammered. "But I can't sing, William. I never have and I never will."

William shook his head. "Wrong, Georgina. Everybody can sing. I'll teach you that too. I've heard your voice and I think you have a beautiful voice. Imagine you can sing those same hymns you've heard me sing."

"I - I ..., don't know what to say," she replied, experiencing a strange, unfamiliar tingling on her skin.

"But you'd love to?" William asked.

"I would, I would, I would; a thousand times."

"I knew it," he grinned. "You talk to Mr. Bartholomew, and I'll pass by later to hear what Mr. Bartholomew has to say about it."

"Thank you. William," she chirped, really meaning it. "I feel like the happiest girl in all of Manchester."

William laughed, showing his sturdy, white teeth. He was adorable when he laughed like that. Still, she wasn't entirely at ease with Isadora's threat and wanted to hear William's reassuring voice on the matter once again. "And ... eh ... you are sure Isadora's father will not make it hard on me? After all, Isadora will probably blame me for what you are about to tell her."

"Don't worry, Georgina. Everything will work out."

He sounded casual, almost a little bit overly confident. But why should she keep on worrying? William knew Isadora and her father lots better than she did, and if he said there was nothing to worry about, she should just trust him. His offer to help her read and sing was among the best things she had ever encountered in her young life, and she should learn not to doubt every good thing that came her way. She forced a confident smile on her face and thanked him again.

"And now," William said. "I will meet with Isadora." His shoulders slumped and his face took on a grave expression. "This will not be an easy talk. I'd much rather sit with you and teach you than to have to face Isadora with her incessant complaining." He gave Georgina an encouraging nod and turned to leave. But just before he let himself out, he stopped and said, "And Georgina...."

"What?"

"It was wonderful that you held my hand. Absolutely wonderful. It was no mistake and I wouldn't mind if you did it again."

Georgina's breath seemed to stop, and she felt her ears getting hot.

She wanted to say something, but nothing came. William turned around and left, leaving Georgina with a whirlwind of thoughts.

William liked her, and she liked William.

CHAPTER 10

When Georgina asked Mr. Bartholomew when she could have her reading and singing lessons later that day, he smacked his lips and his face took on a serious expression.

"William Russell wants to teach you to read and sing?"

"Yes, Mr. Bartholomew, he told me that once I can read, I can read the book of God for myself and he wants me to sing the hymns he has sung. Isn't it lovely?"

"Lovely it is," he said with a sigh. "I just wonder how Isadora Cramps is going to react. You know William is supposed to be engaged to her?"

Just the name Isadora Cramps was enough to make her heart skip a beat. She nodded and said, "I know, Mr. Bartholomew. But it is only reading and singing. Nothing more."

"So you say," Mr. Bartholomew said, but his eyes held a flicker of doubt. "She's a very jealous woman, and she may not take too kindly to you spending time with William."

Georgina resisted the urge to give in to her fears. William had said there was nothing to fear. Should she tell Mr. Bartholomew that William didn't even want to be engaged to Isadora anymore? Better not. It would only make Mr. Bartholomew's concerns intensify. She raised her brows and cast Mr. Bartholomew a questioning gaze. "Can I? I told him I would ask you, since I am now working for you."

She could see a little smile around the man's lips and relaxed. The old caretaker shrugged his shoulders. "You are free to do as you please, Georgina. As long as it doesn't interfere with your work in the church, and you know what you are doing, I don't see any harm in it."

"Really?" Georgina wanted to jump up and felt like flying. "Thank you. Mr. Bartholomew. I will tell William when he comes."

The rest of the day went by quickly and after she had mopped the floor and arranged the hymn books, Mr. Bartholomew told her she could go home and help his wife. But when she came home, Mrs. Brooke wasn't there. There was nothing else to do but to wait until she came back. Maybe, William would already show up. He said he'd talk to Isadora today, and surely that had happened by now.

She imagined how the talk may have gone.

Probably not very well. For Isadora, this was bad news, and she didn't seem like a woman who took bad news gracefully. Pictures of a furious Isadora appeared in her mind, and despite her attempts to shift her focus, the mental images wouldn't go away. Hopefully, William would come soon and then they could arrange their first lesson. *As long as it doesn't interfere with your work in the church*, Mr. Bartholomew had said. That would be no problem. She sat down on the couch in the living room and stared at the paintings on the wall. One painting, of a stern-looking man with enormous sideburns and his hands folded on a Bible, felt a bit uncomfortable. She figured, it was a portrait of Mr. Bartholomew's father, but he did not seem warm like his son. He reminded Georgina more of everything she had ever done wrong. Most unsettling. The other painting, hanging right above the fire place, was different. On the painting, a woman with a tear-streaked face was washing the feet of what must be Jesus. Who else could it be? She had seen pictures of Jesus before, and He just looked like this picture. His hand was on the head of the distraught woman and he stared at her with such warmth and tenderness. That should make everyone feel good. Strangely enough, there were other men in the painting too, but their faces were full of scowls and alarm. Who were they, and why were they so upset?

Georgina felt a connection to the woman in the painting. People looked at her much the same way, and, like the woman, she too felt a deep desire for Jesus and craved for His hand on her head. She would ask William about this story. He would know what it was all about.

Without the sounds of Mrs. Batholomew clattering with her pots and pans in the kitchen and the soft snore of Mr. Bartholomew who so enjoyed stretching out in his favorite armchair, (a seat no one else ever sat in) the house felt strangely empty. In the corner stood a large floor clock, a beautiful shiny piece of craftmanship that smelled of wax and oak wood and recently made her think of heavenly values, rather than the earthly. After all, time seemed to whisk by as quickly as the train heading to Liverpool she had seen once leaving from Manchester railway station. But today, as the golden pendulum swung steadily back and forth, the rhythmic ticking only stressed the emptiness of the house.

If only William would come by. She continued to listen to the sounds outside on the street, hoping to hear his approaching footsteps. But she heard nothing other than the cries of a street vendor, and the high-pitched complaints of a woman calling out to a group of naughty street kids. Little thieves, no doubt, trying to survive any way they could, just like she had for so long.

How strange that you could long for someone so intently after you only knew him such a short time. She never experienced such feelings before.

Finally, she heard someone approaching.

It couldn't be Mr. Bartholomew; he would be home late. Mrs. Brooke, perhaps? That was possible, but Mrs. Brooke was a heavyset woman and these footsteps were of a lighter weight. Then it couldn't be William either. Despite his gentle demeanor, his heavy work boots pounded the ground with every step he took.

The moment the church bell nearby struck three, there was a distinct knock. Loud and hurried, almost angry. Maybe it was William after all. This morning when he had come in, it had sounded much the same. Yes, it had to be William. Georgina got up, ran to the door and opened it wide while shouting, "So good of you to come, William. I asked — "

She stopped in mid-sentence as it had not been William at all who had been knocking. Her stomach churned and she let out a gasp. The mental images, those unpleasant ones about Isadora Cramps, that she had just tried to banish from her mind, materialized. There, right on the doorstep, stood the haughty, icy person of Isadora Cramps. She wrinkled her nose and said, "Well, look who is opening the door. If that wouldn't be our little heart-breaking thief from the slums of Manchester?"

"I-I-Isadora," Georgina stammered. "How good of you to c-come." What a stupid thing to say, but it was the first and only thing that came to her.

"Yes, I thought so too," Isadora hissed. "It's time we set a few things straight. I knew from the very first moment I saw your face you spelled trouble." She snickered and added, "but you wouldn't know what that means since you can't even spell, let alone read or sing."

Georgina steadied herself. She'd been on the streets long enough to defend herself. She had seen bullies before and even gotten into quite a few fights with them. Never were these things fun, but they were part and parcel of survival, and she was not about to be cowered into a corner by this woman who appeared to be an even bigger low-life than she was herself. This was not the moment to show fear. She had done nothing wrong. "She bit her lip and said, "Mr. Bartholomew is not home. Can I leave a message?"

"I am not here for Mr. Bartholomew," Isadora badgered. "It's you I wanted to see."

"Me? Why?"

Instead of answering Georgina's question, she continued her mocking tirade. "Ladies, invite other ladies in," she scoffed. "Obviously, you are not a lady, so I'll invite myself in." Without warning, she pushed Georgina rudely to the side and walked in. As she passed, the potent scent of violets, a costly perfume only the very rich could afford, followed her. Georgina had to admit it smelled lovely, but sadly, the fragrance was only on her skin. It would have been better if Isadora would smell like that on the inside, but that seemed to be only wistful thinking. This woman was not concerned about her inner state, but was on the war path like an enraged savage somewhere in the heart of the Dark Continent, and she had come to settle the score.

Maybe William would show up and save the day. *Please God, let William or Mrs. Brooke come.*

Apparently, Isadora knew her way around as she stepped directly into the living room and plunged herself down in Mr. Bartholomew's seat, the one that was strictly reserved for him.

"What are you doing here?" Georgina demanded, not caring any longer how she sounded. "Get out what you want to say, Isadora." She braced herself for bad news and even worse complications, ranging from being thrown out immediately, getting involved in a common street-fight, or being hauled off to prison by Constable Crowley. But the whys and wherefores were still a great mystery.

Isadora however wasn't about to put her cards on the table. Instead, she tilted her head and said with a stony look, "I have my tea with milk."

"Tea? You want tea?" Georgina didn't understand.

"Of course, I want tea. Tea is what we drink here in Manchester. Or is ale perhaps your preferred drink?"

"Sure. I make tea," Georgina answered woodenly. She felt anger rising, but was still enough in control to say nothing. She could easily make Isadora a cup of tea. At least, it would give her a moment away from the woman and give her more time for either William or Mrs. Brooke to show up.

"Hot tea with lots of milk," Isadora said haughtily.

Georgina turned and made her way to the kitchen. She got the fire going, put on the kettle and got out the teapot. Would Isadora want sugar, too? Maybe it would be best to put salt, lots of salt, in her cup. The thought felt good, but she realized it would solve nothing. Maybe it was better to ask her if she wanted sugar. Two scoops, perhaps one, or none. With a frustrated sigh, she turned and stepped back into the living room. "Do you use sugar too?"

Isadora was no longer sitting in her seat, but stood near the bookcase that stood right next to the floor clock, and was staring at the painting of Mr. Bartholomew's father. It seemed to Georgina that the man didn't like Isadora either. The solemn scowl on his face looked even more severe.

"Would you like some sugar?" Georgina repeated.

Isadora cringed as if she was being caught doing something she wasn't supposed to be doing. It surprised Georgina. She had not seen Isadora behave like that before. "Isadora?"

Isadora turned around. "I was just looking at Mr. Bartholomew's books. Are you always sneaking up on people? Now, where is my tea?"

"I'm sorry, I didn't mean to startle you. It's not yet ready. I asked if you take sugar in your tea. Do you use sugar?"

"Of course, I want sugar. Three scoops, but I can serve myself."

The idea of filling her cup with salt became a very tempting one.

Georgina left once more and hurried to the stove. The water was boiling.

Then, and to her great relief, she heard a key in the lock. *Mrs. Brooke. Thank you, dear God.* Georgina took the kettle off the fire and hurried to the door to tell Mrs. Brooke of the unwanted visitor, but she was too late, as she could hear Mrs. Brooke's exclamations of surprise on seeing Isadora.

"Isadora Cramps, how nice to see you! What brings you here?"

"I was in the neighborhood and thought to ask you about the plans your husband has for Christmas. As you know, Christmas Eve is approaching, and I was wondering if I needed to prepare something."

What is she doing? Georgina decided not to let her emotions run away with her. It was best to bring in the tea and play along. Mrs. Brooke could well deal with Isadora.

When she appeared with the teapot, Mrs. Brooke had taken her own seat and her eyes grew wide. "Oh, my stars," she exclaimed, "You surprise me, Georgina. You are an excellent housekeeper. Blessed will be the man who marries you."

"Hello, Mrs. Brooke," Georgina uttered. "I hope you don't mind I took the liberty to prepare tea for our ... our guest."

"Of course, I don't mind, Georgina," Mrs. Brooke replied while leaning forward in her seat in order to pour the tea into Isadora's cup. Mrs. Brooke served herself a hefty cup of tea as well and Georgina was happy, she had resisted the wicked urge of putting salt in the tea.

"Will it be all right if I go to my room, Mrs. Brooke?" Georgine asked as gently as she could muster. "There's still a bit of cleaning to do, and I suppose whatever the two of you need to discuss is nothing of my business."

Mrs. Brooke frowned. It appeared she wasn't all that keen on having to meet with Isadora Cramps either, but she nodded and said, "Of course, Georgina. Maybe later you can help me with the food preparations."

"I'd love nothing better," Georgina answered truthfully. She turned to Isadora, made a polite little bow, and said, "Enjoy the rest of your day, Miss Cramps."

Isadora was just taking a sip of her tea, smacked her lips, and didn't even look her way.

How good it felt to step out of the living room and leave Isadora in the care of Mrs. Brooke. But what had Isadora actually come to say? She had been so angry, so boorish.

Had she come to make peace, she would have acted differently.

As Georgina sank down on the colorful quilt that covered her bed, she let out a frustrated sigh. She had experienced hostility before, but never from someone so powerful.

But what could she do? She was utterly helpless.

Helpless? Mr. Bartholomew had said something about that only yesterday. It had made an impression on her and she strained her memory to see if she could remember.

"Prayer and helplessness are inseparable. Only he who is truly helpless can truly pray. Your helplessness is your best prayer."

If that were true, then there was only one thing to do. Georgina fell onto her knees before her bed, folded her hands, and sought help from God. After all, as far as she could tell, He was the one who had said, *"Fear not, I am with you."*

She was not used to praying, and did not know how to address God, but telling Him of her fears and anxiety seemed the right thing to do. She struggled for a while with her own thoughts and felt incapable of speaking the right words, but at last she felt some sort of connection, and a deep peace came over her.

How wonderful it was to bring all your cares to God and hear Him say that everything would work out all right in the end. God meant what He said. He would not drop her, even though she had very little knowledge of Him and could not even read His words.

"The road shall be long, My child, but it shall not be one step too long for you."

Just like earlier, when she suddenly had that conviction that she needed not to be afraid, she felt lifted on the wings of her childish prayer. What a relief there would be an end to all this. What a comfort that her road would not be too long. There was only One who could talk like that. Tears of gratitude filled Georgina's heart. If God was for her, then who could be against her?

CHAPTER 11

❄

That day, William would give Georgina her first lesson. She was walking on air. Soon, she too could read, and possibly even sing. William had come by the house later the night before, long after Isadora had left, and they worked out where they could have their first lesson. With Mr. Bartholomew's approval, they could use a small study in the church. That way, it would not take too much time away from Georgina's cleaning responsibilities.

He said he'd be there at nine o'clock sharp and then they'd walk together to the church. Georgina's breakfast sat untouched on the table as she bounced into her seat with excitement. Food was the least of her concerns.

"You should eat something," Mrs. Brooke coaxed her and pointed to the bacon and the crumpet, still hot from the griddle that was on a plate before Georgina. "You can't learn anything on an empty stomach. And my husband needs you later."

Georgina nodded, and more to please her benefactor, she broke part of her crumpet and stared at it. "Where is Mr. Bartholomew anyway?" The piece of crumpet disappeared in her mouth.

"He has a meeting with Pastor Plundell. You'll meet him at the church."

Georgina nodded, but her heart was not in the conversation. "Can I ask you a question?" she asked when she had swallowed the cake.

"Speak," Mrs. Brooke replied with a smile.

"What actually did Isadora Cramps want yesterday, or would you rather not tell me? She was so rude to me and I am afraid she blames me for William breaking off the engagement."

Mrs. Brooke thoughtfully stirred her tea. "It was strange. After you left the room, she only asked a few unimportant things about the Christmas Service tomorrow. Nothing that she couldn't already have known. Then, as soon as she had finished her tea, she got up and left."

"I think she wanted to hurt me; she was angry and rude."

Mrs. Brooke frowned. "That's quite an accusation. After all, you and William are not romantically involved…" she paused and cast Georgina a stern look. "Right?"

"Oh, yes, Mrs. Brooke. There's nothing going on between the two of us. But Isadora called me such horrible things."

Mrs. Brooke sighed and played with her tea spoon. "This world is getting to be such a strange place," she said at last. "The love of so many seems to grow cold. I hope our Savior will come back soon, so we are done with all that anger and hate. In God's Kingdom, there will be no place for all these silly accusations."

Georgina thought about what Mrs. Brooke had said. She had never heard of a time where there would be no more hatred and anger, but that sure sounded wonderful. She needed to ask William about that too. But as far as silly accusations … The things Isadora had called her were not just silly. They hurt.

The clock in the tower nearby struck nine. William would come.

"Can I get ready, Mrs. Brooke?" Georgine asked, but before she got an answer, there was a commotion outside their front door. Voices, mostly angry ones. Then there was a knock on the door. Urgent again, as apparently all knocks were.

"What's all that?" Mrs. Brooke said.

"It … eh … must be William," Georgina said, hearing the uncertainty in her own voice. "Shall I open the door?"

Mrs. Brooke nodded, and Georgina ran off to see what the commotion was all about. "Who is there?" she asked, not just wanting to throw open the door, but hoping to hear the warm, melodious voice of William.

It was not.

A gruff, dark male voice answered. "Open the door. It's Constable Crowley. I want to talk to Georgina."

If someone had punched her in the head, the effect could not have been greater. Her fingers trembled when she opened the door and her heartbeat went twice as fast. She had thought of the constable many a time after her first encounter with the man. Constable Crowley stared at her with an ominous look. If it had not been so scary to meet the constable, she would have laughed, for he looked sort of ridiculous in his uniform, which was too tight. Whether his swallow-tail coat was simply too small for him, or the man was too fat for the coat, she could not say. The rabbit-skin high top hat was barely clinging to his forehead, and his Wellington boots were caked with mud, a far cry from the polished image of the Manchester police force. But none of that mattered to Georgina. She'd been on the streets and had seen worse. What mattered was that he wore the uniform, and that uniform scared her half to death. What was more, he recognized her and surely remembered his promise of locking her up if he'd ever see her again.

But that was not all.

Constable Crowley was flanked by Isadora who stared at her with a victorious grin. Her expression was that of a cat who had been promised mice for dinner and Georgina knew full well who that mouse was.

And there, in the back, behind the bulky figure of Crowley, stood a pale-faced William. Apparently, they all had bumped into each other at the same time; William came to give Georgina her first lesson, but Isadora and Crowley were here for a very different reason.

"So, we meet again," Constable Crowley spoke while he made himself look intimidating and large again by raising his shoulders and baring his teeth. He looked like an angry, oversized bulldog that desperately needed to be put on a diet. "I told you; I know the likes of you. And today, I am arresting you."

"You can't," William shouted. He pushed Crowley, and Isadora aside. Her angry protests didn't seem to faze him and he took his place right next to Georgina. "She's innocent. She didn't steal anything."

"Yes, she did," Isadora fired back. "We want to go in. We'll find the proof."

Georgina's mouth felt so dry it was as if she hadn't had water in a month, and a pain shot through her chest. They thought she had stolen something? She had, of course; but that had all been in the past. But since she had been in the house of Mr. Bartholomew, she hadn't stolen a thing. Did Isadora have some sort of proof that she stole something before? Unlikely. She'd never seen her before.

"Who is at the door, Georgina?" The concerned voice of Mrs. Brooke rang through the hall, and a moment later, the caretaker's wife joined the little group on her doorstep.

"Good morning, Ma'am," Constable Crowley said meekly, and tipped the rim of his hat with his fingers in greeting. "I am afraid I am here on official business."

"It's all a lie," William shouted, but nobody paid him any attention.

"Why don't you all come in," Mrs. Brooke said in a calm voice. She opened the door all the way and invited them all in. Crowley stamped the muddy snow off his dirty boots and followed Mrs. Brooke inside. The others fell into step behind him. Georgina, still trembling from the shock of being accused of thievery, came last. She closed the front door and then hurried after the others to the living room.

Isadora sat again in Mr. Bartholomew's seat. Georgina could see the irritation on Mrs. Brooke's face. Crowley and William remained standing.

"So, what's this all about?" Mrs. Brooke began.

"It's my diamond ring," Isadora burst forth. "I still had it when I came in here for tea yesterday. But now it's gone."

"You may have lost it," William rasped. "You have lost things before."

"No, I haven't," Isadora snapped back, and pointed an accusing finger at Georgina. "She took it. I know it. And good Constable Crowley thinks so too."

"That's right," Crowley agreed, while casting Isadora a warm, faint smile. It disgusted Georgina. The man was like putty in Isadora's hands. "My good mother always taught me that once someone is a thief, they'll always be a thief. I would like to search the premises."

"What?" Mrs. Brooke objected. "Why? Has anyone seen Georgina steal something? She's changed. She's no longer the girl she used to be."

Crowley lifted one hand in the air. "I respect your opinion, Mrs. Brooke, and I hope you are right. But that's why a search would be necessary; but, as I said, once — "

"— A thief, always a thief," William grunted as he interrupted Crowley.

"What's your diamond ring like, Isadora?" Mrs. Brooke asked.

"It's beautiful," Isadora pouted, and her red lips trembled a little. "It's golden with a tiny stone. My father gave it to me when I became an adult. Oh, I miss my precious ring so much."

Mrs. Brooke let out a deep sigh. "Go ahead, Constable. You can search, but only you." She flashed Isadora an angry look. "The rest of us ... well, I suppose I'll offer you all a cup of tea."

Georgina's heart was still pounding. William stood nearby and as Constable Crowley began his search, he whispered, "Are you all right, Georgina?"

She shook her head and whispered back, "I haven't stolen anything. They won't find a thing."

"Of course," William replied, so soft that no one but Georgina could hear.

"Well, there's nothing here in the living room," Crowley said after a while. He turned to Mrs. Brooke who was just coming in with a tray of tea and biscuits, and asked, "Where's the girl's bedroom?"

"First door on your left," Mrs. Brooke pointed him to the hallway.

Crowley walked out and left the others in suspense. The silence was deafening. The only sound that was heard was the occasional slurp from Isadora. She was the only one who wanted tea.

Another fifteen minutes later, Crowley returned. He pressed his lips together and made a helpless gesture with his hands. "Nothing. Of course," he said, "a ring is so small that it will be hard to find without a more thorough search."

"Yes," William snorted, "and the search will be even more challenging if there isn't even a ring."

"There *is* a ring," Isadora wailed. "I just know it, just like Constable Crowley knows it."

The constable nodded. "I aim to please, Miss Cramps. The search is not yet over."

"Have you checked the pockets of her overcoat?" Isadora's cries echoed through the room, reaching an almost hysterical pitch. "I imagine thieves like her will want to get rid of the ring as fast as possible and sell it for a good price to some other low-life."

"Good point," Crowley said, and he asked where Georgina's overcoat was. When Georgina mumbled it was hanging in the wardrobe, he left again.

William clenched his jaws, and turned his anger to Isadora. "What are you trying to accomplish, Isadora? I've never seen you like this."

"What do you mean by, what I'm trying to accomplish?" she fired back with angry eyes, that were now almost as dark and round as the buttons on Constable Crowley's uniform. "Well, I just want my ring back."

At that moment Crowley returned, a victorious smile plastered on his plump face. "Now look what we have here," he gloated. "Look what I found in the thief's coat pocket."

Georgina stared dumbfounded at the chubby hands of the police officer and was almost overcome by a feeling of dizziness and weakness. The floor underneath her feet swayed, and if it hadn't been for William to grab hold of her, she would have fallen over. For there, on the palm of Crowley's hand lay a shiny, golden ring with a stone that sparkled in the light of the morning sun.

"My ring," Isadora exclaimed in a frenzy as she jumped up. "I knew it. I just knew it." She ran up to Constable Crowley and, for a moment, it looked like she was about to hug the man. But just before she did, she thought the better of it and stopped while snatching the ring out of his hand.

"Thank you, Constable," she said and cast the man a grateful smile. "I knew I could count on you."

Crowley's face shone luminously, and he nodded with approval. "But," he said, "there is more."

He looked at the others and asked, "Does anybody miss this?" He opened the palm of his other hand and he revealed an elaborate, silver pocket watch.

Mrs. Brooke gasped. "T-That's my husband's. It's the watch Bishop Clutterson gave him on his deathbed. Where did you find it?"

"In the little thief's coat-pocket, Ma'am," Crowley replied. "It's a small wonder I caught it, as she would have surely sold both items today." He turned to Georgina, a condescending scowl on his face. "That will be prison for you, little lady. So much for your gratitude towards your benefactors. But as I said, 'once a thief, always a thief.'"

"I stole nothing," Georgina croaked, but the words wouldn't come out as her throat was so dry. It appeared only William heard it.

Constable Crowley morphed back into his role of the angry, stuffed bulldog and he stepped forward, wanting to grab Georgina's wrists. But he had not counted on Georgina's years on the street. She was a skilled escape artist and as she saw the dark man coming, she pointed to the ceiling while crying, "There!"

It confused Crowley just long enough. He hesitated and looked up. It was a fatal mistake as Georgina ran past him, threw open the door of the hallway where she took time and grabbed the coat she had gotten from Danyell, and not even a second later, everyone heard the outside door slam shut.

❄

Isadora screamed and dropped her precious diamond ring in confusion. Constable Crowley let out a thunderous howl and yelled, "I will get that Cherry." He sprinted towards the door, but had not counted on William, who just put his right foot in a place where he should not have placed it.

The Constable immediately lost his balance, landed on his pot belly, and rolled over the floor until he came to a standstill near the floor clock in the corner. He lay still for a moment, then heaved himself up and glared at William in anger. "Why did you do that?" he rasped. "You are obstructing the law."

"I am so very sorry, Constable," William spluttered. "You were so fast; I just didn't see you coming. I did not mean to trip you."

"Never mind the chase," Crowley grumbled and wiped the dust off his uniform. "She's long gone. These Hornswoggles know the streets of Manchester better than any of us. No. I'll be on the lookout, and I will catch her another day." He turned to Isadora, who had just found her ring again and was getting up from the floor herself. He told her, "She'll be in jail before Christmas, Ma'am. You can count on our police force."

"Sure," William thought in anger, "With a floozer like you, we have little to fear."

But what now?

He was sure Georgina had not stolen a thing. She may have been tempted, but she hadn't done it. That much was sure. He looked at Mrs. Brooke. The old woman seemed in shock as she clenched the pocket watch in her hand. Would she believe Georgina was innocent? One thing was certain, this was going to be an unpleasant Christmas. He did not feel like singing in the church anymore. Not if Georgina was somewhere out on the icy streets. He needed to find her and make things right. He looked at Isadora. She had set this up. How, he could not tell, but he was sure she'd done it to spite him for having broken the engagement. How could anyone be so wicked and mean? And how was it possible he had not seen it earlier?

"I think we should all go home now," Constable Crowley said. "I think we've caused poor Mrs. Brooke enough trouble for the day." William agreed, as there was not much else to do.

Once they were back on the street, and Constable Crowley took off, Isadora walked up to him. "You see it now, William?" she said in velvety tones. "You can't trust these people. They are from a different class. Do you think … well … can we try again? I'll forgive you for your angry words, and the brewery still needs you."

"Not in a thousand years," he replied, and briskly turned around. He needed to look for Georgina, and was not in a mood to waste more time on Isadora.

CHAPTER 12

Georgina stormed through the streets as fast as her feet could carry her. Away from Isadora Cramps and Constable Crowley; away from being accused of thievery, and away from the shame of having lived on the streets for so long. She could never shake her past. It would always stay with her like a leech that had irrevocably attached its slimy physique to hers and was zapping her hope, strength and happiness. Once a thief, always a thief ... But that statement was wrong. This time, she had stolen nothing. This time, she was the victim of deceit herself, a target of Isadora's terrible contempt and envy. Oh, how she hated Isadora. Yes, she did. She despised her with a perfect hatred.

In her blind escape, not knowing if Crowley would be on her tail, she kept running. She almost collided with a street vendor who, in a raucous voice, was offering rat poison, she barely dodged a lady coming out of a store with a toddler, but things went awry when she crashed into a chimney sweep who had just set his ladder against the red bricks of a mansion. The man rolled over onto the pavement and cursed loudly. Georgina cried her apologies, but couldn't stop to help him up.

Run, girl. Run! Constable Crowley is coming.

At last, she came to a halt in the old part of town, completely out of breath. She propped herself against a dilapidated wall, overgrown with grass, and panted heavily. Suddenly, she realized she was in her old stomping grounds, not too far from where she had grown up and had spent most of her miserable life.

She knew all the cracks and crannies here, the secret little alleys, and the best places to hide. Here she would not have to be afraid of Constable Crowley, but here lurked other dangers. This was the domain of the likes of Uncle Doyle and Paddy Slobcrude and running into them would be almost as bad. No, she could not stay here either. Where could she go?

To Danyell? As soon as she thought of him, she discarded the thought. What could he do? He was still living with his father.

Get out of Manchester.

That made sense. In Manchester, she was vulnerable and in danger of the police and Uncle Doyle. Constable

Crowley would tell the entire police force to be on the lookout for her. No, she needed to get out of Manchester.

She would take the train.

She'd never been on a train, but she'd seen them and trains rode everywhere, even as far as Liverpool or London. She didn't have any money, but that shouldn't be a problem. She would sneak into a freight car and travel along unseen, far, far away from Manchester. Once she was out of here, she would figure out what to do next.

After she had rested a while, she began her trek to Manchester station. She'd been there before. A busy place with lots of people walking about, and while she herself had never done much thievery here, she knew the place was rife with pickpockets and other unsavory types. How strange she had once been among them, and while she was now fleeing like a common criminal, she no longer felt any affinity with her former cronies. She was grateful she still wore the clothes Mrs. Brooke had given her, and while the coat she had gotten from Danyell looked a bit odd on her, she knew she no longer stood out like a beggar girl and would not attract undue attention.

While making her way onto the platform, her heart thumped in her throat. It felt as if she stood in front of a gate that promised to lead to freedom and adventure, although she wasn't entirely sure she wanted the adventure part.

Now what?

A black steam locomotive before her was spewing out dark clouds of smoke and fog, and made strange hissing sounds. The wagons were partially covered in a layer of soot, and the oily, steamy aroma of burned coal stung her nose. So, this was the scent of freedom.

What if she just jumped on, right before departure? It would be easier than having to look for a freight car where she may have to wait for hours, while all the while still being in Manchester.

"Are you going to London?" a cheerful voice behind her asked. "You mind giving me a hand?"

Georgina turned and stared into the flushed face of an older woman carrying several packages. It appeared she almost collapsed under the weight.

"This train goes to London?" Georgina asked.

"Of course," the lady said with a frustrated sigh. "I am about to see my brother's family for Christmas." A small package that had been balancing on top of several other packages in her arms fell off and landed near Georgina's feet. "Let me help you," Georgina said, and stooped down to retrieve it, relieving the woman of another present that was also on the verge of falling. "Thank you," the woman spoke warmly, "but let's not dilly-dally here. We must get on as the train is about to leave." Without wasting another second, she climbed on, apparently expecting Georgina to follow.

Georgina hesitated. Should she jump on, too?

In the distance, she saw a uniformed man approach. The conductor? Or was he a police-officer, looking for her? She had to take a chance, and hoisted herself up onto the train as well. The woman on her way to London sat down at the nearest seat and let out a victorious sigh. "Made it. Thank you again," she said and invited Georgina to sit next to her.

Seated next to the window on the opposite side of the cramped aisle of the train was an individual resembling a laborer, a farmer or perhaps a shepherd, as he was holding a simple shepherd's crook. He had planted his snow caked boots firmly on the floor while casually leaning back in his seat, an amused smile around his bearded face. When Georgina cast him a curious stare, his eyes lit up, and he asked in a gentle voice, "London? On your way to London?"

Georgina gave him an uncertain nod and promptly seated herself next to the woman who was on her way to the Christmas party at her brother's place and avoided the man with the shepherd's crook.

The uniformed man she had spotted earlier passed by the window, and Georgina's heart skipped a beat. A peeler. A policeman indeed. His eyes darted around in search of criminal activity and all Georgina could do was pray the fellow wouldn't board the train as well. Had Constable Crowley already alerted the entire police force of Manchester? It was not likely, still her heart pounded so loud, she feared the lady in the seat next to her would hear it.

"Never been on a train before?" the lady asked, clearly wanting to talk. "You seem a little nervous." A large grin appeared as she babbled on. "You should have seen me the first time I was on a train." She broke out in a hearty laugh. "I was on the brink of losing control of my bladder."

"Yes, Ma'am," Georgina replied half-heartedly while following the policeman with her eyes. "I've never been on a train before." Good, the officer wasn't climbing on board.

"Trust me," the woman incessantly prattled, "Trains are absolutely marvelous. So, you are on your way to London too? I bet you are going home for Christmas to see your family."

"Yes, Ma'am," Georgina obediently responded, longing for the woman to stop her incessant chatter. At that instant, she heard a loud whistle, and instantly the train moved.

"Here we go," the woman cheered. "London, here we come."

Georgina experienced a clammy sensation of cold sweat, and shivered. She was sure a conductor would come, and she had no ticket. While the woman kept talking about all the lovely Christmas gifts she had bought, Georgina kept peering around for a sign of the conductor.

"Still nervous, huh?" the woman asked. "Trust me, you'll be fine." After these comforting words, she broke out into a long explanation about the lovely wooden doll with movable parts that could be operated with a hand crank and that would surely send her nephew, six-year-old Minty Scrubs over the hills. She mentioned the jumping rope for Olivia Scrubs, who had just recovered from Scarlet Fever, talked about the set of toy soldiers for James Scrubs, who was now nine, and about the massive bags of marbles for the whole family. Just when she wanted to explain the Christmas present that she had bought for her brother, Georgina's heart skipped a beat. There, in the distance, still a good number of seats away, she could see the conductor coming.

She turned to the woman and asked, "Sorry, ma'am, but … eh … is there a bathroom on the train?"

"A bathroom?" the lady exclaimed, her voice carrying across the train. Other passengers turned to look. "You really are nervous, aren't you, dear? They should have told you to go before you boarded."

The conductor came closer.

"I'll go see anyway," Georgina said. "Maybe there's a place near the back."

"We *are* near the back," the woman said. "I tell you, there's no bathroom on the train to London. Can you keep it up till Birmingham?"

Georgina shot a helpless stare at the farmer occupying the seat across from her, yet he remained silent about the whereabouts of a bathroom. All the while, the conductor came closer.

The train slowed down.

Georgina could not believe her luck. They rolled into a small station, and through the window she saw a sign flash by. Timperley Station.

Then the train came to a stop. Thank God. Saved by the bell.

"You can't get out here, dear," the woman cried. "We only stop here for a minute or two. You will miss the train and then it will be no Christmas for you in London."

Georgina didn't care. If she didn't get off here, it could be Christmas in jail. She'd never heard of Timperley. While she was still very close to Manchester, it was far enough away from Constable Crowley and Uncle Doyle, and that was all that mattered. Without looking back, she stepped towards the door, opened it and jumped onto the platform. An icy wind whipped into her face. It felt colder here than in Manchester, but for now, she didn't care.

She was in Timperley and could finally relax.

❄

Timperley was nothing.

A hamlet so small, Georgina could hardly believe it. If she had been here on a leisurely trip, she may have loved the place. A quaint little village, right in the middle of a forest with pretty brick houses, stores with windows decorated with the customary holly and pine cones, and snow-covered fields and trees that made for a perfect world.

But she did not come as a tourist.

She came with an empty stomach as a fugitive with no idea where to go. Her belly growled, something it hadn't done for all these days since she'd been at Mr. Bartholomew's place. Given her days on the street, she was no stranger to hunger, but now, this nagging emptiness came to her as an irritating surprise. She needed to get used to it all over again. Her days of crumpets, eggs and bacon, hot chocolate milk, and bread with real butter were over. She wished she had not been ignoring her breakfast that morning while waiting for William. But alas, there was no use crying over spilled milk …

As she strolled through what appeared to be the main street, her thoughts drifted back to Manchester and to

William. What would William be doing now? Tonight was Christmas Eve. He'd said it was their big night at the church. He'd be singing, Pastor Plundell would speak again, and afterwards there would be food. Lots of it.

This was supposed to have been her first truly joyful Christmas Eve ever, but things couldn't look any bleaker. She pulled up the collar of Danyell's winter coat as high as she could and shivered, on the verge of tears.

Now that the initial danger had ebbed away, and there was no need to run any longer, the awful reality of her situation dawned on her. No roof above her head and no food to nourish her. Thoughts of God and His care, wonders she had supposed had been proof of His goodness, were far away. In fact, her heart was almost as cold as the weather outside, and her fragile newfound faith was under attack.

Was Uncle Doyle right after all by claiming faith was a big hoax, a means to keep stupid people stupid? Isadora, that horrible witch, went to church and she, too, sang those same beautiful hymns William had sung. What good was faith in God if you had to sing praises to Him while joining hands with people like Isadora? She might as well go back to Uncle Doyle since there really wasn't that much of a difference. She had told God she would steal no more, but relieving some unsuspecting person from his purse seemed the only option left. After all, this was an emergency. But how? In this miserable town hardly anybody was out, and if she even succeeded in stealing, she didn't know the hiding places and the place was so small she could not buy food anywhere without being recognized as the thief.

No. No. No. She was done with that old life. She would *not* go back to it. Something Mr. Bartholomew had said came to her. What was it he had said? *As a dog returns to its vomit, so fools repeat their folly.* She was no dog, and didn't want to be a fool, either.

At the edge of town, she spotted a large stone near a junction. Maybe she could rest awhile. She was so tired. Suddenly the misery of the day pressed on her shoulders like a big boulder and she felt she had no energy left. If she could just rest for a moment and think about her options, options she did not have. So she planted herself down and stared dejectedly at the two roads ahead of her. The one she was on led to the forest, while the other seemed to circle back into town.

This was the end. Hopeless. She was finished.

Pray, Georgina.

Why? Prayer didn't seem to help.

Then she thought back on those moments when she *had* truly prayed; times when that warm gentle voice had encouraged her and told her she didn't need to be afraid, because her way would not be one step too long. But the way was long ... So very long. The embers of her faith seemed to have almost flickered out, but these thoughts of God still being around fanned the barely burning coals. Yes, she should pray. There was nothing else to do.

And so she folded her icy hands, closed her eyes and whispered a prayer.

"God, here I am. I am so lost. Isadora Cramps has accused me of theft, but I have not stolen. Now I am here in a strange place, and I am cold and hungry. Will you please hold me? I don't know what to do. Amen."

It was short; nothing special. But it was a prayer. When she was done, she kept her eyes closed and listened intently. Perhaps there would be a voice; perhaps the snow would suddenly melt and warmth would radiate from the sky. None of that happened. In fact, the cold seemed even colder. Yet, the stillness comforted her. She noticed the trickle of a small stream somewhere nearby. The water emitted a soft gurgling sound and deep in the forest, she'd heard the screech of an owl; but no message from God.

And then there were footsteps behind her. Snow crunched under someone's boots and then a voice called out to her. Not in her mind, and neither was it the cry of an angel with a message from God. No, this was a real human voice. "Hello, may I ask what you are doing?"

Georgina turned and gasped. There, in the snow behind her, stood the farmer she had seen on the train. He was leaning on his shepherd's crook. "I - I -," she stammered. "I am sitting down."

"I can see as much," the man replied. "But why are you sitting here on a cold stone in the middle of winter, while you were supposed to be on your way to London?"

Georgina cast him a nervous stare, and for a moment she considered running again. His shepherd's crook looked dangerous. If he would bring that stick down on her head, he could cause considerable damage. Maybe she wasn't supposed to sit here, and the people of Timperley considered this stone sacred or something. By sitting on it, she was dishonoring it. But his eyes seemed warm and understanding, and it didn't appear he was about to hit her at all. Oh, why was all this so confusing? She was so tired, and did not want to run anymore.

That's when the tears came. "I don't know why I am sitting here," she blubbered, feeling awful to show herself so weak. Surely, the man with the shepherd's crook would laugh at her and tell her to get lost.

But that didn't happen. Instead of mocking her, he threw his shepherd's crook down in the snow and regarding her with pity he bent over and he gently touched her shoulder. "Surely, it can't be that bad," he said. "Why did you jump off the train?"

"Because I didn't have a ticket to go to London," Georgina wailed. "I am not going anywhere."

"Mercy me," the man replied while raising himself again. He heaved a sigh of concern. The cold temperature caused his breath to resemble smoke. "You can't stay here. You'll freeze to death. What happened?"

Georgina looked up. He did not appear to be dangerous, although his shepherd's crook was. Why would anyone carry around a shepherd's crook in the middle of winter? At this point, she hardly trusted anyone. But what did she have to lose? Things couldn't get much worse.

"I am running away," she said at last, hoping the man would not get angry.

He did not.

Instead, he thoughtfully pulled on his beard and then said, "I see." Georgina was prepared to hear his sharp rebuke, urging her to move on, but to her surprise he exclaimed, "It's Christmas Eve. Not a night to be sitting out in the cold while most folks enjoy their festivities. Tell you what …," he paused. "My farm is not much of anything, but it's warm and I have some food. You can stay the night."

Georgina blinked her eyes. "S – Stay the night? W - Why are you being nice to me?"

He shrugged his broad shoulders. "As I said, it's Christmas Eve. It's that precious moment in the year when even the most wicked individuals concede to a small burst of tenderness in their hearts. How could I let you sit here on a stone in the middle of winter? Something tells me I should open my door to you."

"But Christmas is supposed to be a family feast. Maybe your wife won't like you bringing home a stranger?"

"Don't worry about my wife," the man replied with a chuckle. "Tonight, it's just me, myself, and nobody else." A slight smile played around his lips when he said, "Unless you are dangerous. Should I be worried about taking you in?"

"No - No, Sir," Georgina said, "I am not dangerous at all."

"I know you are not," the man replied. "But just so you know, I've no decent bed for you in my house, but you can sleep comfortably in the barn together with Lissie, Beulah, and Easter Bell."

"I thought there was nobody living with you?"

"Well, no humans, that is. But Lissie is my cow, Beulah is my donkey, and Easter Bell my lamb. You got any problems with that?"

"No Sir, not at all."

"Then let's go. By the way, the name is Bear."

"Bear?"

He chuckled. "That's what people call me here. I've been called differently, but Bear will do. What's yours?"

"Georgina Castle," Georgina said.

"Well then, Georgina, let's get you to a warm place." Bear picked up his shepherd's crook, shook the snow off, and took the path that led into the forest.

CHAPTER 13

"The lodge," Bear explained, as he guided Georgina over the path to his humble dwelling, "is my forested Eden; it's my sanctuary where I withdraw from time to time."

"So, you normally live elsewhere?" Georgina asked.

"I do, but I am glad I am here today so I met you." As he walked on, half leaning on his shepherd's staff, he looked up and said, "Every day, the magnificence of the forest makes me realize how great our heavenly Father is. Wouldn't you agree?" He turned to Georgina and his eyes shone with little lights of happiness.

A lump formed in Georgina's throat. She forced it down with a gulp. She'd never been in a veritable forest. The closest she'd ever come to any resemblance of a forest was the park, not too far from the harbor. *His forested Eden?* It was something William could have said. She did not need to be afraid of this man. Would he sing too, like William? "Yes, Mister Bear," she replied politely, not quite knowing what else to say.

He chuckled. "You don't have to call me Mister Bear. Bear will suffice."

"All right, Bear. Where else do you live if you are not here? London perhaps?" she said, as she stepped over a snow-filled pothole. She had to be careful not to sprain her ankle.

"I've been to London. Actually, I get around quite a bit," he said. "Manchester doesn't hold secrets for me."

"It doesn't?" Georgina said. Would Bear know the area where she had lived most of her life? Should she ask him? But then, as if he could read her mind, he said, "I know the area near the canal really well. Old Manchester, with places like Angel Street ... you know it?"

Georgina blushed. "Yes, Sir ... I mean ... yes, Bear. That's where I grew up." Instantly, images of her past rose and filled her mind. Uncle Doyle's beatings, Paddy Slobcrude's disgusting selfishness, her running away from the police ... A tinge of nausea rose. She rubbed her forehead with her palm.

Bear seemed to notice her anxiety as he said in a warm voice, "But that is the past, isn't it? You are not there anymore."

No, she was not.

"You don't have to go back there anymore," Bear said with a tone of finality as if he could tell. Of course, he was just talking. What did he know about her life? At least, thanks to him, for tonight, she'd be safe … But, what about tomorrow?

Bear stopped and pointed to a small clearing in the forest. They had arrived at his farm. Clearly, he had not said too much. It didn't look like a farm at all, rather it resembled a meager shack. Sturdy, efficient, but nothing special. Just four wooden walls with a door, a chimney, a few windows, and a roof that seemed to sag and sigh under an enormous mound of snow. Behind the shack was a bigger structure; no doubt the stable. It was clear why Bear wanted her to sleep in the barn. There just wasn't any room in the house. The farm was a small, one-room house that doubled as a kitchen, living room and bedroom. The stable seemed a lot more spacious. Sleeping with a cow, a donkey and a lamb would be quite an adventure, and something she'd never done before, but to her, it made no difference. She was grateful. Considering the alternative, fighting off the cold on your own in an icy forest, anything was a blessing.

"Come on in," Bear said. "Make yourself at home."

He stepped inside, and Georgina followed him, expecting to see something that would remind her of her days at Uncle Doyle's. Clutter, empty liquor bottles, dirt and a general mess. After all, a man living by himself was apt to be corrupted by the company he kept.

But she was in for a surprise and she gasped. The fresh scent of pine filled her nostrils and, for a moment, visions of what it would be like in the country house of the likes of Queen Victoria entered her mind. The place was small, and yet it appeared to be strangely spacious. And, it was crispy clean. There was no clutter at all; no bottles, no sweaty, unwashed clothes and socks scattered over the floor, and no selfish mess so prevalent in her former dwelling. Georgina instantly felt at home and breathed a sigh of wonder. Everything exuded a refreshing beauty. The furniture, consisting of a table, a few chairs and a modest seat tucked in a corner, was simple but inviting. Positioned in the opposite corner was a brick stove, next to a pump. Apparently, Bear even had running water. Directly next to her was a well-crafted bed, featuring a gorgeous, colorful quilt showcasing a collection of singing angels. Almost best of all, there was a comforting fireplace with gracefully swaying flames that radiated a pleasant warmth. Had that fire been burning all that time when Bear had been in Manchester? Wasn't that a bit careless, or did Bear have a friend who had lit the fire before he got here, so he wouldn't be cold upon arriving?

It didn't matter. All that mattered was that she was safe for the night.

When she looked up, she noticed several sturdy cross beams that ran across the ceiling and fortified the room. No, this place wasn't about to cave in. A lot more snow would have to fall before this cottage would collapse.

"You seem surprised?" Bear asked.

Georgina pressed her lips together. "Well ... eh ... it looks lovely in here. The outside looked so plain, so I had not expected such loveliness."

"The outside is functional. But it's my understanding, the inside of a thing is always more important than the outside."

Georgina didn't understand and raised her brows.

"People," Bear stated with a knowing smile. "Many people are beautiful on the outside, but inside their dwelling is not so pretty at all. To me, unpretentious simplicity on the surface and authentic beauty underneath is more desirable than striking beauty on the outside and ugliness inside."

Georgina nodded. That sounded about right. If only she too could have true beauty inside. Her outside appearance was already very plain and not pretty at all, but there was nothing she could do about it. But how did she look on the inside? She wasn't too sure.

Bear welcomed her into the room with his hand and told her to sit. Georgina gratefully sank down on the seat against the wall. Bear picked up several logs and added them atop the dancing flames. He rose from his crouched position by the fire and inquired, "What time would you like to have your meal?"

Eat? She was famished. "W-When do you usually eat?" she asked.

He looked at her with a smile. "I know that look on your face. You must be hungry." Before she could even answer, he went on and said, "We can go to the table at any time."

Georgina looked at him in amazement. Bear made it seem like her presence was absolutely normal, almost as if he had expected her long before, and he made her feel like she was his guest of honor. She really didn't understand any of it. But Bear apparently did. He looked at her as if he knew exactly what was going on in her head, and said, "You stay put. I'll make you a nice hot cup of tea and when you are all warmed up inside, you can help me set the table."

Georgina jumped up. "I can help now, too."

"Not necessary," he said. "You just relax. It's been a harrowing day for you, and tea will help."

Georgina yielded to his request. She leaned back in the seat and saw how Bear prepared her a large mug of tea and not a minute later the hot liquid warmed up even the coldest fibers of her being. This was wonderful. Bear was right. This day had been horrendous, but for the first time since Constable Crowley had knocked on the door that morning, she felt completely at ease.

Bear retreated to the kitchen counter and began fiddling with pots and pans in preparation of the meal. Georgina sat back in rest and peace. The sound of dear Bear cutting vegetables plus the warmth of the open fire made her feel drowsy. Her breathing became slow and steady and all of a sudden, without realizing it, she dozed off into a deep, restful sleep.

❄

The flames of the wood fire warmed Georgina's cold limbs, and she moved as close to the fire as she could without hurting herself. It was a chilly night. All nights were chilly, but here, close to the fire, it was pleasant. In the distance, she heard the bleating of sheep. The sheep did not need the warmth of the fire. They all had their own sweaters and winter coats. Still, the bleating startled her. Why did she hear sheep?

It was obvious. She was a shepherdess in the fields, and that's what shepherds and shepherdesses do; they take care of their flock. There was nothing strange about it. Her sitting on a coarse blanket on the barren desert ground near a fire was the most ordinary thing in the world. She noticed her fellow shepherds. Rough men, dressed in simple clothes. Some were trying to sleep. One giant fellow snored so loud it was almost comical. But she was right at home here. Everything was just as it was supposed to be.

Just as Georgina tossed another stick into the fire, a bright light appeared in the sky.

A light? Was that a new star, and why had she not seen it before? As she looked at it intently, it appeared to grow bigger and brighter. Georgina got up and peered into the heavens. Yes, it *did* grow in size and brightness. The other shepherds had seen it as well and were excitedly pointing at it while letting out startled cries and looking for a place to hide from whatever terror was coming their way. Strangely enough, Georgina felt no fear. Rather, she welcomed the light. Somehow, she knew this was something good. While the light was now intensely bright, it didn't blind her at all. Then it stopped growing in size and stayed in place, hovering several yards above the flock of sheep, while bathing the entire country in a mesmerizing brightness.

No fear. Even the simple sheep didn't seem to be alarmed.

Georgina narrowed her eyes so she could see better. Was it true? Was something materializing right in the middle of the light?

Yes, there was.

In the center of the light, a being appeared. A heavenly being revealed itself to them.

Georgina's heart pounded. Was that an angel? It had to be. They were standing in the presence of an angel who was traveling in a vehicle of radiant beauty. At that moment, Georgina fell to her knees in awe. Behind her, she heard other shepherds cry for mercy. The one that was always snoring had woken up too, and was seeking shelter behind a bush. Then the angel spoke; loud and clear. His words rolled out like ... no, not like thunder. Thunder was scary, but while his words were almost deafening, yet they were filled with an unearthly tenderness.

Fear not: for, behold, I bring you good tidings of great joy, which shall be to all people. For unto you is born this day in the city of David a Saviour, which is Christ the Lord. And this shall be a sign unto you; Ye shall find the babe wrapped in swaddling clothes, lying in a manger.

Suddenly there was with the angel a multitude of the heavenly host praising God in song. A chorus of celestial beings harmonized in praise of God, heralding His greatness and His compassionate desire to grant mercy and to bring peace to men of good will.

Oh, what beauty. The song they sang didn't just gently touch Georgina's heart, but unleashed such a wave of emotion that she couldn't hold back her tears. She lifted her hands into the air as far as she could and stretched out her fingers, hoping to grasp some of that light; to take hold of the beauty and the pureness of something so divine and to carry it with her for the rest of her days. And so, she sat with her arms outstretched and her eyes now closed, for she did not know how long, until someone touched her shoulders.

She opened her eyes and looked back. It was one of the shepherds. She recognized the snorer, who had gotten ahold of himself and had come out of his hiding place. He now beckoned to her. "The angels have departed," he stated the obvious, as the plains were as dark as before, possibly even darker, since the fire had almost died down. "We need to do what the angel told us. Will you come with us to Bethlehem and see this thing which has come to pass, and that the Lord has made known unto us?"

"Yes, a thousand times yes," Georgina replied. "But how shall we find this place?"

The snorer pointed towards the heavens and said, "Look, there's a star I have never seen before. I think we are supposed to walk toward the star."

It sounded just about right, and after they had prepared the sheep, they all walked in the direction the star seemed to be pointing. Georgina walked along with them over the plains and hills towards Bethlehem. All the while, her heart was singing and dancing.

When they reached the top of a hill, she was the first one to see the stable.

A hovel, really. A shack. It was a desolate sight. Just a ramshackle construction, badly in need of fixing up. But it had to be the place the angel had told them about, for it appeared the star pointed right at it.

How these things were possible, Georgina did not know, but that didn't matter to her at all. Once you have seen an angel and an entire choir delivering the most beautiful music you have ever heard, you question nothing. You just take everything in and you revel and bask in the beauty and holiness.

"What do we do now?" one of the shepherds asked.

"Well, it's obvious what we will do," Georgina answered. "We knock on the door and we'll go in." Without waiting for anyone's approval, she stepped forward and did as she had said. Her fingers trembled and her heart pounded as she let her hand come down upon the door and knocked.

At first, she heard nothing, but then the door opened and a bearded man appeared. He said nothing, but when he saw the shepherds, he stepped back and motioned for them to enter, almost as if he had expected them.

It was rather dark inside, but a small lantern emitted light into a fraction of the stable.

Near the back, in the shadows, she saw the silhouette of a donkey. Apart from the gentle bleating of sheep, it was totally still, as if a holy hush rested on the stable. That made sense. The angel had spoken of the birth of the Savior, and what could be holier than that?

Then she saw the baby, lying in the arms of a woman with a blissful smile on her tired face. She looked up just as

Georgina stepped forward and, for a moment, they looked at each other. The woman nodded as if to welcome Georgina. She hesitated.

There, the Savior of the world in a stable? It was just a baby in a barn, surrounded by cattle, and the place didn't seem to be all that clean; just a rough barn that smelled like a farm, and yet she instinctively knew she was standing on holy ground.

Of course, this was holy ground. An angel had sent them here. No, she was the witness of a miracle.

Most intriguing of all was the baby itself. What a pretty face the little guy had. She couldn't see the color of his eyes, but it looked like he was smiling at her as if he was happy to see her. So small, so tender and ... so helpless. Was that really the Saviour of the world? In holy awe, Georgina stepped closer.

She heard the other shepherds following her and from the sound of their feet, she knew they were thinking similar thoughts.

"This baby is called Emmanuel," the woman said in a barely audible voice. "That means 'The Lord is with us.' But we will call him Jesus. Do you want to hold him?"

Georgina shuddered. "H-Hold him? But he is so tender; so fragile. What if I hurt him?"

A smile appeared. "You won't hurt him." Without waiting for Georgina's response, she moved and lifted the baby towards Georgina, who took the child, wrapped in swaddling clothes, and held him close to her. As soon as she took the babe in her arms, a deep sense of peace, a blissful deliciousness, washed over her. A glory she could not put into words, but it filled her heart with unspeakable words and music.

A desire to sing rose within. She wanted to sing. Yes, she should sing. Some unfamiliar urge compelled her to just open her mouth and let the words roll out. She'd never done anything like it, but here, in the stable while holding the baby that the angels had been singing about, she let the words come out, just as she felt them —

"— It's time to wake," a gentle voice sounded close to her ear. "The food is on the table. You slept a long time."

Huh, what food?

The stable, the shepherds, the baby … they seemed to vanish and for a moment, Georgina didn't know where she was. Then, she stared into Bear's eyes and when she saw him and the happy, dancing flames behind him in the open fire, she realized she had been dreaming.

"I-I am sorry," she said while rubbing her eyes. "I must have dozed off, but I had this dream, this most wonderful and amazing dream."

Bear gave her a little smile. "I know," he said. "You were moving your arms around and I didn't have the heart to wake you, but just now, when you began to sing, I figured it was best to wake you."

Georgina cast him an incredulous stare. "I sang? No wonder you woke me up; it must have sounded horrible."

"On the contrary," Bear said, "You have a beautiful voice."

"Why then did you wake me up?"

"It was time," Bear said with a gentle smile. "Food is getting cold."

Georgina shook her head and continued to rub her eyes. "Oh, Bear, it was so lovely. In my dream, I was a shepherd girl. There were angels, and we went to see the barn into which the Savior was born."

"So you dreamt about the Christmas story?" Bear asked and his eyes were twinkling.

"Yes, I think so. A few nights ago, I heard about the genuine Christmas story for the first time, but I never knew it was so beautiful."

"It was beautiful," Bear said. "Most people *know about* the Christmas story, but they don't really *know* the Christmas story."

"I - I don't understand?" Georgina asked.

Bear grinned. "You've heard about Queen Victoria. You know about her, but you don't really know her, since you've never met her and you don't have a relationship with her."

A light of understanding dawned on Georgina's face. "It was all ... so holy," she mumbled.

"I know," Bear stated simply.

"But ... eh ... what did I sing?" Georgina asked.

"A Christmas carol."

Georgina shook her head. "Impossible. I don't know any Christmas carols. In fact, I know no songs."

"But you did." Bear grinned and softly sang in a rich and deep voice:

> *For lo! the days are hast'ning on,*
> *By prophet seen of old,*
> *When with the ever-circling years*
> *Shall come the time foretold*
> *When Christ shall come and all shall own*
> *The Prince of Peace, their King,*
> *And saints shall meet Him in the air,*
> *And with the angels sing.*

When he was done, a deep silence fell over the room. At last, Georgina mumbled, "I sang that?"

"You sang another couplet. I just finished it."

Georgina recognized the song. It was the one William had sung that night when Danyell had accompanied him on the violin. "William was going to teach me to sing, but I didn't know I could sing."

"You are talking about William Russell? I know him. He's quite a gifted singer. He'll be a good teacher for you."

Georgina tilted her head. "You know William?"

"Of course, I do," Bear replied with a chuckle. "But I tell you, you are a gifted singer too. You'll make a good couple."

Georgina blinked her eyes. "Wait … what are you talking about?"

Bear just motioned for Georgina to come and sit. "Let's eat, Georgina. Cold food on Christmas Eve is not customary."

Georgina got up, but something had changed. Her fears, her depression, her tiredness… they were all gone. A deep sense of rest took their place. Bear was not just an ordinary farmer. There was something about him she couldn't describe, but she didn't dare ask him about it. She smiled, pulled out her chair and sat down to the most wonderful meal anybody had ever served her.

❄

It was hard to fall asleep that night. So much had happened that day, and so much was still happening. It had been a baffling, but most wonderful day. It had already started early that morning. She thought back on the breakfast she didn't have with Mrs. Brooke. That had been the time when she still looked forward to William's arrival and his first lessons. Reading, writing, singing... The heavens were about to open. But that had not happened. Instead, the ground had opened and ugly monsters in the form and shape of Constable Crowley and Isadora Cramps, armed with horrendous lies and accusations, had crawled out and had done their utmost to finish her. She had to run again, as she had done all her life. The train had brought her to Timperley, of all places. She had never even heard of the place and it had seemed like a big mistake. What had she been thinking? How did she think she'd survive the night without money or shelter? Certainly, people would have found her frozen dead the next morning if it hadn't been for Bear who had taken her in and fed her. What a special man he was.

And then that dream...

And now she was lying in the hay, surrounded by Lissie, Beulah, and Easter Bell, the lovely cattle of Bear. The animals were extremely friendly and didn't seem to mind she was lying there at all. In fact, the soft braying of Beulah was a blessing and only enhanced her excitement of sleeping in a barn on Christmas Eve.

Jesus was born in a stable, so she was in good company. For some strange reason, Bear's stable looked a lot like the stable she had seen in that lovely dream, but that was probably because all stables look alike. After all, they were all just places to keep the animals safe, warm and dry. Jesus had been in Mary's arms and was wrapped in swaddling clothes. There were no arms to hold her, but she was wrapped in Bear's majestic quilt; the colorful one with the singing angels. Despite her objections, he had removed it from his own bed and insisted she use it for the night. She hadn't even been *that* comfortable in Mr. Bartholomew's house. This place was so cozy and warm that she wouldn't have minded settling here permanently.

Of course, she could not, and Bear had made that abundantly clear as well.

Outside, tree branches were lightly scratching against the stable. The wind had picked up and was howling its icy, mournful song. But her heart was no longer mournful. What a special night it had been.

To Bear, everything seemed business as usual. When she told him she had never experienced a day like today, he just shrugged his shoulders. "Christmas is the time for wonderful things to happen," he stated with the air of somebody who explained to a child how to butter his bread. "Good things always come to those who believe in Christmas. When Christmas praises are in the air, our Father above performs his mightiest miracles."

After the meal, when they had sat near the fire, the conversation had grown more serious. He had served her a cup of hot chocolate milk and then sat down with a serious look on his face. "Georgina?" he said, his voice significantly more serious than it had sounded throughout the entire day.

"Yes, Bear?"

"Whatever it is you are running from," he said, while folding his hands, "You need to go back tomorrow. Back to Manchester."

"T-To Manchester?"

"Yes. You can't stay here." He had looked at her so intently that Georgina felt he was looking straight through her. "This ..." He added thoughtfully, "... is the wrong path."

"I understand I can't stay with you, but going back to Manchester ..." Dread filled her heart. "Couldn't I get a job here in Timperley? Surely, you must know some farmers I can work for." As she heard her own voice, she knew she sounded ridiculous. Who would hire a runaway? Manchester was full of paupers, and nobody wanted some of that destitution in Timperley.

"The choice is yours, Georgina. It always is, but this is not leading to where you want to be."

"But they have accused me of things I've not done." She cast him a pleading glance. Surely Bear would understand her. He would not want her to go to the Manchester jail. Suddenly, the hot chocolate milk, that had tasted so nice before tasted bitter. She put it down, lowered her eyes and mumbled, "I hate Isadora Cramps, and I am afraid of Constable Crowley."

"I know," Bear said. "Hate and fear are the black spots on your gracious heart. You need to give them up."

"I tried to," Georgina blurted out. "There have been moments I felt sorry for Isadora, but when I saw her this morning and I heard the terrible things she said, I couldn't take it anymore." Tears stung her eyes. Why did Bear have to talk about such things? Things had been so wonderful with the dream and then the luscious Christmas dinner ... why could Bear not keep his mouth closed and not bring these things up? Georgina remembered all the other ugly things Isadora had called her. Maybe Bear would understand it better if she told him all the names she had called her. She looked up and, while wiping a tear off her cheek, she balked, "It was not the first time, you know. You should have heard the terrible things she called me before. You know what she called me? She said I was —"

"— I know it's hard," Bear interrupted her calmly, "but forgiveness is what Christmas is all about." He leaned forward and said, "Do you really think that God will let you fall into the brambles when you do the right thing?" And then he said something that gave Georgina goosebumps. He said, "Fear not. You are in My hands."

The very words God spoke to me when I was praying. She fixed a wide-eyed stare on Bear. "What did you just say?"

He smiled. "I said, 'Fear not. You are in My hands.' That's in the Bible, you know. It's God saying it, and it's my understanding that if God says something, we can just trust that word."

"S-So," Georgina stammered, "you think I need to go back to Manchester and do what?"

"I don't know," he said with a grin. "That's for you to find out. But that's the walk of faith, and I believe it's the best way to get your heart cleansed from that ugly dark spot of hatred that is growing in your heart."

Georgina stared at Bear and realized her mouth had sagged open. Who was this man? How was it possible he knew so much? But in spite of all her own objections, one thing was crystal clear. He was right. If she wanted to be happy again, and free from all this fear and hate, she needed to do as he had suggested. It would be hard, but it was the only way.

Soon afterwards, Bear said he was tired and he helped her to get settled in the barn. That must have been hours ago, but it didn't matter. She was too excited to sleep. She'd been without sleep before. Yes, tomorrow she'd go back to Manchester. Tomorrow she'd face the music and see what God would do. A song welled up in her heart, a gentle melody, and Georgina began to hum it. It was the

Christmas Carol William had sung, and as she mumbled the first lyrics, she finally fell asleep.

CHAPTER 14

Lissie was mooing when Easter Bell let out an excited bleat, and Beulah gave a cheerful bray. The animals seemed to be in a cheerful conspiracy to wake Georgina up, and it worked wonders. She instantly pried open her eyelids and sat upright, scanning her surroundings in bewilderment.

A stable?

Then she realized where she was. She was at Bear's place and after his wonderful Christmas dinner he had put her in his warm barn, where she had slept under the magnificent quilt with the singing angels.

Beulah stared at her with his faithful donkey eyes and let out another hee-haw as if to say, "Get up, sleepyhead. It's Christmas morning. The sun is up and life couldn't be more beautiful."

Georgina smiled at the donkey. "Good morning to you, too." She pulled off the quilt, yawned and stretched her arms. A jubilant ray of the morning sun beamed in through the window and causing a veritable feast of dust particles frolicking in the brightness.

Beulah was right. It was a beautiful day. Georgina adjusted her attire and plucked a few strands of hay from her hair, wondering how long she had actually slept. It couldn't have been for very long. She'd been so excited about all that had happened that day that sleep just wouldn't come.

And today she would have to go back to … Manchester. She had made peace with the idea, although it wouldn't be easy. As she unlatched the door of the barn and bid the animals farewell, she wondered if Bear had a few more surprises for her up his sleeve.

As she stepped outside onto the freshly fallen snow, she marveled. Yesterday, upon arrival, she had seen how pretty the area was, but now, breathing in the fresh, crisp morning air, and stepping onto a fresh layer of snow that scintillated and sparkled with joyful brightness in the sun, she understood why Bear had called it 'his forested Eden, his sanctuary'.

Here, away from the noise, the filth, and the confusion of Manchester, it almost seemed like you could touch God. But alas, she had to leave.

Bear's little farmhouse was steeped in silence.

Would he be awake? She hated to wake him up, but judging by the risen sun, it was high time, and thus she gently knocked.

No answer.

"Bear?" she cried in a loud whisper, hating to disturb the stillness that cloaked the area like a divine shroud of heavenly beauty.

Still no answer.

She pushed on the door, and it swung open. "Bear?" she cried again. "Are you decent? I am coming in." She gingerly opened the door all the way and entered the room, praying that the old shepherd wasn't lounging near the stove in his skivvies.

He was not. In fact, he was nowhere. Since the farmhouse was comprised of only one room, she could see immediately that Bear was not around.

A generous amount of freshly baked bread was on the table, accompanied by cheese, haddock, and cured meat. Next to it was a small pouch, resting on a picture of a train, pointing to a group of houses. Georgina's fingers trembled as she touched the pouch and lifted it off the drawing.

The meaning was clear.

Bear was gone, and he wasn't coming back soon. He left her food and money for the train to Manchester. She marveled as she picked up the pouch and checked its contents. There was more, much more than the price of a ticket to Manchester. Tears pricked her eyes. What kind of man was Bear, anyway? She would not have to jump off the train to avoid the ticket conductor, or lie and steal to make her way back into Manchester.

She clutched the money pouch to her heart and while looking at the ceiling, she whispered, "I am coming back, Bear. I'll repay you every cent."

❄

It must have been in the early afternoon when the train came to a halt at Manchester station with its loud screeching wheels. The locomotive emanated a suffocating plume of smoke that enveloped the platform. Georgina stared out the window and waited inside until the air had cleared somewhat. Then she jumped off the train. The first thing she saw was a peeler, a police man, standing near the exit. He surveyed the station with eagle eyes; his feet firmly planted on the ground and his hands casually folded behind his back. Yesterday, his presence would have terrified her, but not today. She was no longer afraid. God had promised her He would be with her every step of the way. Regardless of whether that path led through a dim valley or over a bright mountaintop, it was all the same to her. There was nothing to be afraid of.

She passed by the peeler and couldn't help but give him a bright smile. "Good day to you, Sir," she said. He eyed her for a moment with a curious look, then beamed her a smile of his own, and tapped his hat in greeting. "And to you, Ma'am."

Georgina just walked on, cheerful and her heart full of grace and gratitude. This Christmas day was without equal.

As she exited the station, she stopped. Where to now?

To Mr. Bartholomew's place? Perhaps to Danyell and his father, or even more daring, ... to William and his parent's house? None of these options gave her a sense of peace.

No, it was best to go to the church. Even though it was Christmas day, it was improbable for a service to take place right now. Services were usually in the morning or in the early evening, but somebody would be there. She would have to take it one step at a time.

The idea gave her peace. Going to the church from here would mean she had to go through the poor part of town. Taking the route through Angel Street was by far the fastest. Of course, she could take a detour, just to be sure she wouldn't bump into some folks who knew her, or even worse, into Mister Paddy or Uncle Doyle. But a detour would take a long time.

She pondered her options for a moment and then dropped the idea. She'd walk fast through Angel Street, and keep her head down. What were the chances of Uncle Doyle or Mister Paddy being out? Uncle was probably sleeping off his hangover, and had God not told her not to be afraid? No, she'd be fine.

And so, she stepped away from Manchester station and headed for Angel Street.

❄

Paddy and Doyle had terrible headaches. They'd had them all morning, and as far as Paddy knew, they would last the rest of the day. Maybe, if they would get something decent to eat, or possibly have another drink, then he could subdue his pain. Of course, it was all the fault of the inferior liquor they were now drinking. Not that the stuff they drank before was all that good, but now, with Georgina gone, the stuff they'd been drinking these last days was close to poison.

That was all Georgina's fault. If only she had not run off.

Doyle was still slouched on the ripped couch, his legs hanging limply over the edge, and his eyes sealed. He didn't want to get up and Paddy knew all too well not to push him. Didn't they say 'Let sleeping dogs lie?' That was certainly true for Doyle. The fellow was susceptible to fits of rage, and especially when there was a headache involved, he was liable to lose his temper and act recklessly.

It hadn't been all that long since Georgina had run off, but already life was becoming more strenuous. That horrible, repugnant and disloyal shrimp. Paddy grunted. She had been a good thief, at least, a better one than he or Doyle would ever be. Of course, even with Georgina's help it hadn't been a feast. They never had enough money to stop working; never enough to stay home for a few days, or to enter the land of no worries like those rich *dimber-dambers* did; people who carried themselves with a haughty air of superiority, parading in their extravagant outfits with their noses so far upturned to the sky they could almost cut through the clouds.

Horrible. Unfair. Life was unfair; it always was, and particularly so during Christmas, when everyone crooned about nothingness, indulged in lavish dinners, and frittered away their time in attending meaningless church services.

If only they could get that wicked Georgina back. They would teach her a thing or two and then things would be better again. Of course, she would be back eventually. One day, she'd wake up, longing for her former life. Who did she think she was, anyway? If you were born for a dime, you would never be worth a quarter, and that was all Georgina was, a sickening, rusty dime.

Paddy sighed and rubbed his pounding head. Complaining about Georgina would not get them anywhere. She wasn't here. If they wanted something to eat or drink, he had to go out and get it. "Doyle," he shouted, "I'll hit the streets."

No reaction.

Paddy secured the rope tightly around his torn pants and let out a deep breath. The forthcoming afternoon was going to be arduous, but one must do what's necessary. Yesterday, he had stolen nothing, and there was a good chance that today it would not be much better. "Bye Doyle," he murmured as he opened the door. "Whatever I get today is for me and myself only."

As he stepped out into the muck and the mire of his alley, he cringed. Colder than he thought, but at least the biting cold helped his head not to hurt all that bad. He turned left toward Angel Street. Everything always started at Angel Street. From there, he would figure out where to go. Maybe he would come across some intoxicated individual who had attended a Christmas party, and couldn't defend himself. Then, this was going to be his lucky day.

When he turned onto Angel Street, his heart skipped a beat. Did he see correctly? He blinked his eyes a few times to make sure he wasn't hallucinating, and then focused on what he saw. He saw a woman … And she looked just like Georgina. She wasn't dressed in rags which made him doubt he was right, although her coat looked somewhat strange. It looked more like a man's winter coat. But the way she walked, her gait … only Georgina walked like that.

He stealthily trailed her and became convinced. There was no mistake possible.

Yes, this was his lucky day.

He would follow her and once he knew where she was hiding out, he'd get Doyle. He licked his cracked lips and chuckled. "Now we got you, you little shrimp."

His headache was totally gone.

❄

Georgina walked as fast as she could through Angel Street without causing undue attention. She had the collar of her coat pulled up as high as she could, held her head down, and only allowed herself to relax a little when she reached Ashley Lane and the turnoff point from where she was to make her way to Manchester Cathedral and the church on the side.

She had not really expected any unpleasant encounters with some of her former buddies; and yet one could not be too confident. After all, she virtually knew this area like her inside coat pocket and so did all her former associates. Like her, when she was still in *the business*, they were constantly on the lookout for anything out of the ordinary that could bring them some ill-gained profits.

But nothing happened. Nobody spotted her and she was fine. All went well, and while she still kept a low profile, she made her way through a myriad of streets and alleys until, at last, she saw the Cathedral rise in the distance. Next to it was the door that led to the sanctuary that had become so dear to her in only a few days of time.

The place seemed deserted.

No people thronging in and out. No one discussing the Christmas service, and nobody licking the last crumbs from their lips after having feasted on Mrs. Brooke's muffins and Christmas bread she would have served after the Service. But that was to be expected. It was no time for a Service. All she hoped was for the right person or persons to still be around.

Who? She did not know. She came here by faith, hoping God would show her what to do next.

She walked up to the door and pushed on the handle as she had done that first night. It opened again, and she stepped inside the dark hallway. This time she heard no singing as she had done when she first met William. But there were voices.

Yes, somebody was still there. Would that be Pastor Plundell? She had never spoken to him personally ..., Maybe, it was Mr. Bartholomew, getting the place ready for the evening service.

Unexpectedly, the peace that had carried her all the way from Timperley to here, seemed to falter. Nervousness bubbled up inside and the old familiar urge to run stuck up its ugly head again.

No-no-no. She gritted her teeth. Running away was a defeat. It would solve nothing. God had promised He'd be with her. And just so she would not give her rising panic a chance to take the upper hand, she pushed on the door to the sanctuary and stepped inside.

Several candles that she herself had placed there were burning, and the rich scent of pine branches filled the air. Instantly, her fears subsided. Even if there wasn't a concrete passageway to heaven in any of these churches, as she had previously thought, God was here and that was all that mattered. That meant safety, hope, and closeness to the truth.

Two people; a man and a woman, were sitting together in the pews, not too far away from where she stood. They hadn't noticed her yet.

Who were they? That wasn't Mrs. Brooke, although it was difficult to see as she could only see her back. And the man … it looked like Danyell. Could it be?

She narrowed her eyes and then noticed the musical instrument that was resting on the pew next to him. A violin. Yes, that man was Danyell.

Georgina felt like calling out to them, but something stopped her as Danyell and the woman were involved in a deep discussion. Despite it being rather unladylike, she couldn't resist eavesdropping on their conversation. She perked up her ears.

"You need to set this straight, Isadora. You are ruining someone's life." That was Danyell, and he was talking to … Isadora.

That woman, sitting with her back to her, was Isadora. There was the woman who had made her life so miserable all over again. She felt rage rising. She could grab a nearby candlestick and hit that horrible woman over the head with it. That would serve her right…

Instantly, the words of Bear came to mind. *"Hate and fear are the black spots on your gracious heart. You need to give them up."* The dark thought she had just entertained, scared Georgina, and she shuddered.

Oh, that old man was right. Bear had read her heart perfectly well. The thought that had crossed her mind was absolutely dreadful. While Isadora had been unspeakably bad and wicked, she herself should never again yield to such thoughts of rage and hatred. It would solve nothing and only make matters worse a thousand times.

God was in control; He would take care of matters. His will for her was to let go of that dark, black spot in her heart and to forgive even Isadora.

Isadora answered, and Georgina listened. "You don't understand it, Danyell. She has bewitched William. William no longer wants to marry me. It's all her fault."

As Georgina heard that dreadful voice, some strange sensation welled up. No, a candlestick was totally out of the question. That woman needed something very different. She needed warmth, kindness … forgiveness

Huh…

Though she couldn't fathom how, and where these thoughts came from, she saw it so clearly. Instead of anger filled with resentment and justification, a sense of benevolence for the woman emerged. That woman was desperate. Without knowing it, Isadora had fallen prey to the deceitfulness of riches. Self-centeredness governed her life and egotism sat on the throne of her heart. But seeing her through the eyes of God, she too was like a lost sheep on a faraway hill, groping around in darkness and holding on to all the wrong things for security. She and Isadora were much alike.

Would she walk up to them and see if peace was possible?

Danyell spoke again. "I know you planted the stuff in Georgina's coat, Isadora. Don't deny it. Do you really think that this is the way to gain William's favor? The police are looking for her and she may go to jail for it. Have you no conscience?"

"That's easy for you to say," Isadora snapped back. "She's just a street girl. These folks know how to survive in prison. If she hadn't shown up, I would still marry William. It's just not fair."

"*You* are not being fair, Isadora."

Isadora didn't budge. A smirk appeared on her pretty face. "Will you tell William that you think I planted those things? There's no proof I've done anything wrong."

"No, Isadora, I will not tell him. I don't think I need to. He's more than capable of making up his own mind. But…, he paused, "… as far as proof is concerned, Somebody has the proof. After all, 'The eyes of the Lord are in every place, beholding the evil and the good.'"

"What is that supposed to mean?" Isadora barked. "Is that a threat?"

Georgina heard Danyell sighing. Had the situation been less grave and had she not been the focal point of the turmoil, she would have even smiled at the ridiculousness of Isadora's answers. But what could she do about it?

"Of course, that's no threat, Isadora," Danyell replied calmly. "But we both know you are lying. This is Christmas. This is a time of forgiveness; peace on earth to man of good will. You've been here singing words like: Truly He taught us to love one another; His law is love and His Gospel is Peace. Chains shall He break, for the slave is our brother. And in His name, all oppression shall cease."

Georgina listened intently. Even Bear could not have said it better. What would Isadora say now?

At that moment, a side door opened, and Mr. Bartholomew entered. Georgina looked back and stared into the surprised caretaker's eyes. He looked at her, bewilderment on his face, and then exclaimed in a loud voice, "Georgina ... what are you doing here?"

Georgina cringed, and Danyell and Isadora jumped up. Chaos erupted.

Isadora's shrill yell echoed through the church as she pushed Danyell over and yelled, "She heard everything. She heard us talking."

"Heard what?" Mr. Bartholomew called out from afar. But Isadora just rushed forward and bolted out the door, leaving the others behind in a state of confusion.

Georgina ran after her.

She needed to stop Isadora. She wanted to tell her that everything was all right. It was Christmas and this was not the time to fight and yield to hatred and misery... If Isadora would continue on the road she was on, it would lead her to untold misery and pain.

CHAPTER 15

"Isadora, stop," Georgina cried out and stormed after Isadora. "I mean you no harm." But Isadora didn't stop and kept on running as if a group of bloodhounds were on her trail.

Georgina struggled to keep pace with her. She hadn't expected Isadora to be so fast in her lavish, wide and flapping clothes. Women's fashion was not designed for such activities as running and sprinting, and she prayed Isadora would soon be out of breath. "Isadora, stop!"

Still, she ran.

They were quite an amusing spectacle for the people on the street who smilingly mimicked them and joked about angry, unfaithful women fighting over a man's heart. As she shot past the cheering, mocking bystanders, she thought wryly that all those ignorant people weren't even that far off. After all, the reason Isadora hated her that much was because of a man.

"Stop!" Georgina kept crying. "Let's talk about this. Please."

As in a flash, she noticed they were coming to the poor part of town. Not the area they wanted to be.

At last, Isadora stopped in a deserted little alley, a place she would never have gone into had she been in her right mind. It was unclear whether she halted because of the shortness of breath or because she was finally willing to engage in conversation with Georgina. Judging by her puffy face and the sweat that dripped from her lovely cheeks, it was probably because she was exhausted. Bent at the waist, she gasped for air, bracing herself with her arms on her knees.

"I - I -," she gasped, but she couldn't finish her sentence.

Georgina came to a standstill next to her. "Isadora," she panted, "Please, I wish you no harm."

Isadora stared at her for a moment from her crouched position. Then her face registered terror.

Terror? Isadora didn't need to be afraid of her.

"You don't have to be afraid of m —" Georgina began, but a roguish laugh from behind cut her off, caused a shiver in her spine and cut through her heart like a knife.

"Look who we've got here? Paddy, you grab that one, while I take the other."

Before Georgina knew what was happening, she felt an iron grip around her wrist and a rough hand turned her rudely around. She stared into the ugly face of Uncle Doyle. "So, you thought you could run off on us, you miserable wretch," he spat.

"Uncle Doyle," Georgina asked in confusion, "W-What are you doing here?"

"Getting what belongs to me with interest," he chuckled while he looked at Paddy who held Isadora. The poor woman, exhausted from her run, had no strength in her to resist and looked around with large, wild eyes. She was terrified.

"Scream, Isadora," Georgina cried out. "Let people know we are — "

Uncle Doyle forcefully covered Georgina's mouth with his coarse hand and tightened his grasp on her arms with the other. She could taste the grime and sweat of his palms. "Quiet, you ratbag. We are the ones in control," He howled.

Georgina still hoped Isadora would scream. Paddy wasn't all that strong, and it was doubtful if he could hold her if she would put up a fight. But she did not. Fear petrified her, and not a peep came out of her mouth.

"We have to get off the streets," Uncle Doyle hissed to Paddy. "Can you hold that Church-bell?"

"She's as putty in my hands, Doyle," Paddy said. His eyes had a strange, subterranean glint and he looked agitated and almost hysterical. "Where are we going?"

"Home," Uncle Doyle snarled. "We'll ask ransom for the woman and we get Georgina to behave. Our troubles are over, at least for now."

So you think, Doyle ... Georgina's thoughts raced at lightning speed, surpassing even her speedy run from before. This would not happen. This had to stop.

Fear not, I am with you.

The thought hit her heart like an arrow, imbuing her with courage and resilience. Yes, God was with her, and nothing was going to stand in his way. Uncle Doyle's wry, clammy hand was still pressed against her lips, pressing her nose down painfully. That had to change.

With Uncle Doyle's hand clamped around her mouth, she pried her jaw as wide as possible and bit down with all her might, ruthlessly piercing his palm. This was not the time for loving behavior. Uncle Doyle yelled and cursed in pain and his hand slipped off Georgina's mouth. The vice-like grip on her wrists eased, and just momentarily, he released her so he could tend to his injured hand. It was all the time Georgina needed. If Uncle Doyle believed the worst was behind him, he was in for a rude awakening.

Not taking any chances, Georgina forcefully planted her feet into his chin. This time, as he rolled over the pavement, he howled like a pig being dragged to its demise in the slaughterhouse line. So much for his wicked bravery.

There was not a second to lose. Georgina turned to Paddy and hissed, "Let her go, Paddy. Now!"

Paddy had always been a coward. Seeing Uncle Doyle crawling around on the ground, crying and whimpering like a messed-up hyena, he shuddered and began to howl, "Don't hurt me. I am only doing what Doyle told me to do. Don't kick me."

But he still held on to Isadora, who seemed on the verge of fainting.

"Let her go," Georgina hissed once more. She had to be fast, as Uncle Doyle was about to crawl back onto his feet and his fury would be terrible. The wicked man crept toward Paddy and squawked, "Don't let her go, Paddy. She is the gateway to a better life."

Paddy affirmed with a nod. Uncle Doyle's words seemed to give him confidence. He squeezed his little eyes together and gasped, "Then get her, if you can, little shrimp."

Desperately, Georgina looked briefly toward the end of the alley. Perhaps somebody was coming and Uncle and Paddy would flee in fear, but she saw no one. Out of the corner of her eye, she saw Uncle Doyle straighten up again.

Something had to happen now. Now, immediately.

Suddenly she pointed her finger at Paddy and Uncle Doyle and cried out in a loud voice: "God help us! Send Your heavenly guard dogs on these horrible men and lock them up in some dark dungeon where they cannot hurt anyone anymore."

The result was shocking.

Uncle Doyle once more toppled backwards, Paddy quivered, and both men emitted a fearful cry. And then, as if there truly was a heavenly hound on their tail, they turned and ran off, as fast as their fearful legs could carry them. Georgina gazed in awe as they vanished from view around the corner.

The ordeal was over. They were safe.

She turned to Isadora, who wept and sagged onto the dirty stones, not caring for her beautiful clothes. "It's over, Isadora. They are gone. The bad men left."

Here sat the mighty Isadora, crying like a child on the cobblestones in a dirty alley. Here was the woman who had lied about her, had tried to put her in jail, and had called her all kinds of horrible things. And all because she blamed Georgina for having stolen William from her. But there was no anger in Georgina's heart. That hatred had left the moment she had truly understood what Bear had meant about that black spot in her heart. Forgiveness was the true meaning of Christmas. What was it again Danyell had said in church?

> *Truly He taught us to love one another;*
> *His law is love and His Gospel is Peace.*
> *Chains shall He break, for the slave is our brother.*
> *And in His name, all oppression shall cease.*

"I am so sorry about your misfortune," Georgina whispered to Isadora while stroking her shoulders. "I wish you no harm. I am not trying to steal William away from you. I just want to learn to read, write, and sing."

Isadora glanced upwards, her face marked by tears, and a teardrop poised on the tip of her nose. "It's me who is sorry," she wailed. "What a fool I have been. I despised you from the moment I first saw you, but …" Her voice trailed off and she didn't finish her sentence.

"But what?" Georgina asked in a gentle voice.

More tears rolled out, and Isadora's shoulders shook. At last, she uttered in a barely audible tone, "You Georgina are a better woman than I am. Will you forgive me? It was me who took the silver pocket watch from Mrs. Brooke that afternoon when I visited you. I took my ring and put it in your coat pocket, hoping you'd go to prison. I hated you for taking William away from me."

Georgina's heart went out to the weeping wretch on the ground, and she put both her arms around Isadora in a tender hug. The sight would have appeared remarkably odd to the jeering, mocking crowd from earlier, had they seen the two women there in the alley on the ground hugging, but nobody was there.

"I barely know William," Georgina said. "I fell in love with his singing, and he's nice. He wants to teach me to read and write, but that's as far as it goes."

Isadora shook her head and even forced a little smile on her tear-stained face. "No, Georgina. He doesn't love me, and he told me so. He loves you. I know him, and I know the way he looks at you. And really, it's all for the best. He doesn't want to be a beer-brewer. He wants to sing for God, and …," she paused, "… so do you. You two belong together; at least that's what it looks like to me." A new tear rolled out of her eye and fell onto the pavement. "I have behaved horribly. How can I ever even sing in church again?"

Georgina tightened her embrace. "What about me, Isadora? You were not altogether wrong about me. That horrible man that attacked us was my uncle. For years, I was living under his reign of terror. I've cheated and stolen more than can be written up in books." A lump formed in her throat and now she too felt a tear building up. "I shouldn't sing about God's goodness, but that is precisely why we celebrate Christmas. Because of the baby in the stable, the gate to heaven has opened, and anyone who wants to can sing about God's love, free from guilt and free from fear."

"Thank you, Georgina," Isadora said barely audible, and Georgina knew she really meant it.

At that instant, they heard running footsteps coming their way.

Uncle Doyle and Paddy? Had they regained their courage? Georgina felt Isadora cringe, but there was no need for fear. The concerned face of Danyell appeared around the corner, followed by Mr. Bartholomew, Pastor Plundell, and … William.

"Are the two of you all right?" Danyell asked as he crouched down beside them.

"Yes, we are," Georgina replied, while tears stung her eyes. "Everything is fine."

"What happened?" William asked as he stared at the strange sight before him.

"Christmas happened," Georgina replied and smiled through her tears. "It's that glorious time of the year when we all need to sing and praise God for His goodness."

❄

That night, Georgina slept in her own bed again, her bed in Mr. Bartholomew's house. She woke up the next morning with the wonderful scent of fried bacon, eggs and homemade muffins, and it made her stomach growl. But there was something else that made her jump out of bed. William had promised her he'd be coming by that morning for their first reading lesson. Thinking back on what had happened to her these last days was indescribable. How was it possible her life had changed so much in the course of such a small amount of time?

She lifted her eyes to the ceiling and uttered a small prayer of gratitude, got dressed and went to see Mrs. Brooke and Mr. Bartholomew who warmly greeted her. The old caretaker smiled and put a cup of hot chocolate milk before her.

The last time she'd been drinking hot chocolate milk had been when Bear had served it to her. How nice it would be to see Bear again and tell him of all the wonders that had happened to her. He had known. Imagine what would have happened if she had not gone back to Manchester, but had pushed her own willful way and stayed in Timperley?

There was a noise near the front door. She was just taking a bite of her muffin, but jumped up. There was the knock she'd been waiting for. "It's William, Mrs. Brooke. Shall I open the door?"

The old woman gave her a gentle nod. "Please do, my child."

Georgina ran to the door and swung it open. But it wasn't William who had been knocking. It was the surly Constable Crowley. For a moment, his presence confused her, but there was nothing to worry about. Or was there?

"Hello Constable. Are you here for Mr. Bartholomew?" she asked, not quite sure what to expect.

"No, I am not," he retorted, yet Georgina detected his uncertainty. "I am here to ask you a favor."

"A favor? Me?" Georgina blinked her eyes. "How can I be of help, Constable?"

He hesitated, scratched his forehead and mumbled a few unintelligible words. At last, he cleared his throat and said, "Let me first say I am sorry that I misjudged you. I heard what happened with Miss Cramps. She told me all that she did and I reckon an apology from me is in order."

Joy flooded Georgina's heart. So that's why he was here. "Well, that's quite all right, Constable. Will you come in for a muffin, perhaps?" She opened the door all the way and made room for the husky man to enter. But he stayed put.

"Well ... eh, no. There's something else I need from you."

"Oh?"

"Will you show me the whereabouts of your uncle and his miserable crony? My orders are to arrest them and send them off to the Manchester jail. Miss Cramps has officially filed a complaint."

Georgina nodded. "Of course, Sir. I understand, but will you allow me to finish my breakfast?"

He smiled. It was the first time Georgina saw him smile. So, he was human, after all.

"In that case," he said, "I'd be most happy to have a muffin."

"Then come in," Georgina said and made room for him to enter. As she was about to close the door again, she saw William arrive. He spotted her at the door and enthusiastically waved. As she saw his gentle face, she remembered the words Isadora had spoken to her: *He loves you, Georgina. I know him, and I know the way he looks at you.*

Georgina's heart started to thump. Did she love him too, or did she only like him because of his singing and his promise to teach her to read and write?

As she saw him approach, she knew the answer. His singing and his teaching skills where nice, beautiful, helpful and necessary, but none of that really mattered.

No, there was the man she would like to get to know, and who knows, maybe, one day, they would marry and have children. She thought back on her dream in which she had been holding baby Jesus. That had been breathtaking, but it had only been a dream. How lovely it would be to hold a baby of her own ...

Then she knew.

Yes, she loved him too.

EPILOGUE

"Where are we going?" William asked as they boarded the train to Timperley.

"I have to settle an old score," Georgina answered.

"In Timperley?" William raised his brows. "What could there possibly be in that little Podunk town?"

"There's Bear," Georgina replied simply.

"Bears? There are no bears in all of England."

"I didn't say bears. I said Bear. He is a man who lives on a farm with Lissie, Easter Bell, and Beulah, his cattle. And he's living in a part of the forest that is so lovely. I would really like you to see it."

Georgina could see the befuddlement in William's mind. "A man called Bear with his animals on a farm in

Timperley? Have you perhaps stolen a good deal of money from that man and now you want to make amends?"

"No, William. I never stole from him," she explained. "He paid for my train fare back to Manchester, and now I want to pay him back. I promised I would. But I also want you to see the sights."

"How did you ever get in Timperley?"

Georgina sighed. "It happened when I ran away that day from Constable Crowley. I never told you where I went that day. Bear put me up. He literally saved my life, and he's quite an amazing fellow. A staunch believer too, and I think you'll like him."

"So, he helped you?"

"He did," Georgina agreed. "In fact, it was at his barn where I had that amazing dream, I told you about when I was holding baby Jesus as a shepherd."

While talking, William helped Georgina on the train and they sat down. William was quiet, probably processing what she had just told him and what was so special about a man called Bear. Once he'd see the place and met Bear, it would all make more sense.

She noticed they were virtually sitting at the same place where she had sat before, next to the lady who was on her way to London. How things had changed since that day, and how wonderful it was that now she was traveling together with William; no longer afraid, and no longer on the run. How good God had been.

The ticket controller came by. Georgina handed the jolly man her ticket and beamed him a grand smile. "A good day to you, Mrs.," he responded as he handed her the ticket back. "Going for a picnic in the forest in Timperley? It's lovely, you know."

"I know," Georgina said while taking William's hand in hers. "But, it's still Miss. Hopefully, soon it will be Mrs. Today, I was just hoping to visit an old friend."

"Ah, I see," the conductor said. "I bet you two are on your way to see Reverend Pickleton. They tell me he's quite the expert on performing marriages."

Georgina grinned. "No, Sir. I have never heard of Reverend Pickleton; but we will visit Bear. I am sure you've heard of him."

"Bear?" the conductor replied with a frown. "No, I can't say I have heard of him. Is he a new arrival to Timperley? I know the place well."

"I think he's been here for years. At least, so he said," Georgina replied. She felt a little dumb, but then looked up and added, "Anyway, thanks for your time. Have a good day, conductor."

"And the two of you," he said as he tipped his cap in greeting and walked on.

The train slowed down.

Already the sign of Timperley showed, and William and Georgina got up.

"All right," William said after they had climbed off and glanced around at the picturesque, quaint station. "Where is Bear?"

"Follow me," Georgina said as she stepped forward and guided William out of the station, into the little hamlet.

Last time she'd been here, it had been so dreadfully cold, but not today. It was not yet Spring, but it would not be long before new life would burst forth, and today, at least, the weather was mild and agreeable. Finding her way was easy. Like last time, all she had to do was to follow Timperley's main street, passing the familiar stone where she had prayed, before venturing straight into the forest.

"It's beautiful here," William exclaimed as they stepped through the forest.

"It is," Georgina said. "It's like a forested Eden."

William's brow went up. "That would make for the lyrics of a good hymn. I should remember that." Georgina did not answer as she concentrated on the path ahead. There were still the same potholes, the lovely stream and there, in the clearing, should be the farm.

"We have arrived," she stated, a little confused.

"We have?" William asked. "I see no farm."

Georgina rubbed her forehead, glanced in both directions. However, there appeared to be no farm or barn in sight. "But this is the place," she said haltingly. She'd been here only one night, but she was certain they were at the right spot. "I-I don't understand," she mumbled. "He must have moved."

William tilted his head. "If there had been a structure here, we should see some signs, dear. But there's nothing here."

William was right. There was no sign there ever had been a farm, let alone a barn. The clearing held nothing but fresh, luscious grass, and strangely enough, the ground was covered with tiny white lilies. There were no flowers growing anywhere else. It was too early and too cold for spring flowers, but here, on the open spot, the lilies were blooming in great abundance.

In the distance, they heard someone whistling a tune. It came from further down in the forest. Georgina's heart fluttered. Maybe that man could tell them what was going on.

Soon after, a man appeared. A giant man with a bushy beard and a warm smile on his face. A German Shepherd dog accompanied him and when he saw them, he stopped, called his dog to sit still next to him, and eyed them with surprise. "Are you folks lost?" he asked. "I can help you. I know the way around here, like my pocket."

Georgina breathed a sigh of relief. *A woodcutter.* Surely this man would know Bear's whereabouts. "Not lost, sir," she said, "Just a little confused. We are looking for Bear. Do you know where I can find him?"

"No bears here, Miss," he replied. "We aren't living in Russia. There's plenty of wild boar here, rabbits, deer ... you name it, but no bears. Not a single one."

"I know that, Sir," Georgina answered, perplexed. "We are looking for Mister Bear. The farmer who lives here and who has a cow called Lissie, a lamb called Easter Bell, and a donkey called Beulah."

The man stared at Georgina as if she wasn't quite right in her mind and then said, "Sorry, Miss. I've lived here all my life. In fact, I got my house just up the path. There're no folks here by that name. In fact, there's nobody in all of Timperley called Bear." He shrugged his shoulders and then said with a smile, "And, if you'd ask me, nobody would ever call his donkey Beulah and his lamb Easter Bell." He plucked at his beard and added, "Lissie is still a good name for a cow. Names are important, you know." He placed his hand on his Shepherd dog and said, "Isn't that right, Wolverton?"

Georgina was speechless. Her hand flew to her chest and she felt her heart racing. She had not imagined it. Bear had been just as real as William and the man and Wolverton all put together.

"Well," the woodcutter said, "if you'll excuse me, I am on an errand. Goodbye." Without further concern for those ignorant strangers, he called his dog and stepped forward, leaving Georgina and William behind.

When he was gone, William turned to Georgina. "Well," he said, "what's that all about?"

"I really don't know," Georgina gasped. "Bear really was here."

William nodded and put his arms around Georgina. "I understand little about it, but judging by the enormous change in your life, I have no reason to doubt that what you told me is true. I guess we'll never know the depth of God's mysteries until we arrive in Heaven and He'll show us all He did for us on earth. God works in miraculous ways and it is well said that his best miracles always happen around Christmas."

Georgina gave him a loving smile, though she was not quite ready to let it all go just yet.

She had not imagined it. Everything about it had been real, including the food, the animals, and the warmth of the fire.

"I have an idea," William spoke softly. "This place is so beautiful and I understand why you call it your forested Eden. I would love to sit for a while among those beautiful lilies and compose a new hymn with you."

"Me with you ... compose a hymn?"

"Yes," William said, "And it will be the first hymn we'll sing together in church."

That sounded lovely. What could be better than to sit in the middle of the forest on a balmy day, surrounded by lilies and composing a hymn to glorify their loving Savior?

"We will give it a catchy name," William said as he placed his coat on the grass for Georgina to sit on. When he sat down himself, he pulled out a pencil and a notepad and wrote in large letters: 'Our forested Eden.'

Right then, Georgina spotted something near the end of the clearing and behind a tree. "Wait a moment," she said. "I see something." She got up and, while she let William ponder about the first lines of their new hymn, she stepped away to investigate.

"William!" she exclaimed with excitement a few moments later. "Come here. You will not believe it."

"What?" William said, but he did as Georgina asked him and got up. Seconds later, he joined Georgina and stared in wonderment at what was lying on the ground before them. It was a quilt. A beautiful quilt picturing a large group of angels with trumpets and singing in glory to God.

"W-Where did that come from?" he mumbled. "Who would leave a quilt so precious in the forest like that?"

"I know who did," Georgina said with a heavenly expression on her face. "Bear did."

※

THANK YOU FOR CHOOSING A PUREREAD BOOK!

We hope you enjoyed the story, and as a way to thank you for choosing PureRead we'd like to send you this free book, and other fun reader rewards…

Click here for your free copy of Whitechapel Waif
PureRead.com/victorian

Thanks again for reading.
See you soon!

LOVE VICTORIAN CHRISTMAS SAGA ROMANCE?

If you enjoyed this story why not continue straight away with other books in our PureRead Victorian Christmas Romance library?

Read them all...

Churchyard Orphan

Orphan Christmas Miracle

Workhouse Girl's Christmas Dream

The Winter Widow's Daughter

The Match Girl & The Lost Boy's Christmas Hope

The Christmas Convent Child

The Orphan Girl's Winter Secret

Rag And Bone Winter Hope

Isadora's Christmas Plight

PLUS THESE BRAND NEW CHRISTMAS TALES
FROM OUR BESTSELLING VICTORIAN
ROMANCE AUTHORS

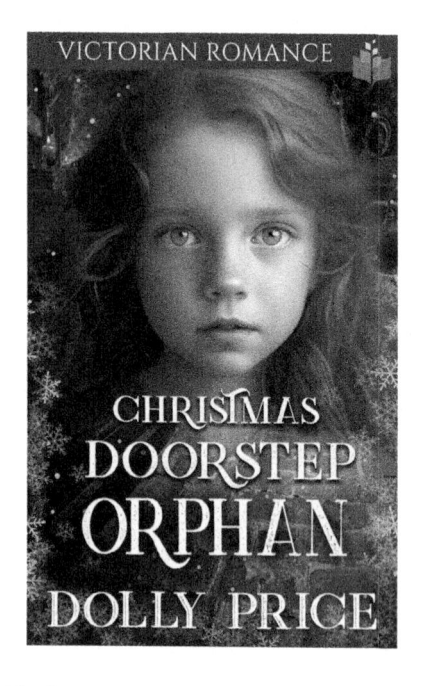

Read Christmas Doorstep Orphan on Amazon

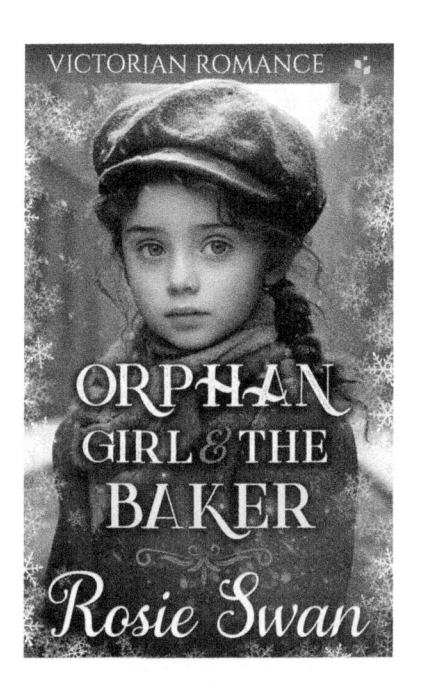

Read Orphan Girl & The Baker on Amazon

Read The Desperate Christmas Angel

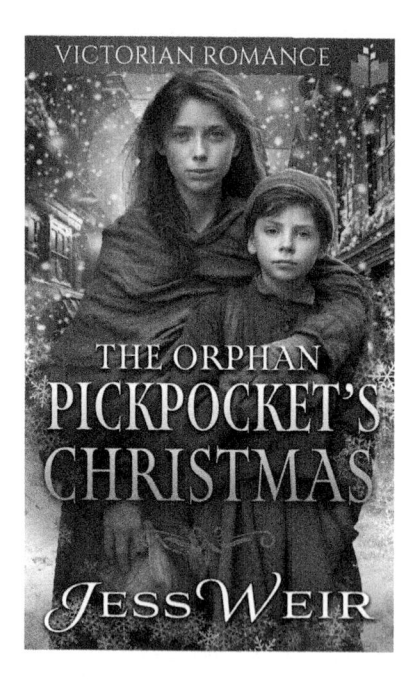

Read The Orphan Pickpocket's Christmas

For your enjoyment one the page you'll find the first chapters of Christmas Doorstep Orphan, a story you are sure to love...

HAVE YOU READ?

CHRISTMAS DOORSTEP ORPHAN

Now that you have experienced the wonder of 'A Christmas Song For The Prestwich Orphan' why not dive straight into another unputdownable Victorian Romance?

If you enjoyed the courage and romance you witnessed in Georgina's story you are sure to fall in love with Dolly's other bestselling seasonal tale, *Christmas Doorstep Orphan*.

This story begins on a frosty Christmas Day. An unexpected arrival shakes the opulent world of the Leigh-Donner family in Belgravia. A mysterious note claims the abandoned child is their kin, but they're reluctant to embrace her as their own…

What will happen to little baby Emma?

You'll not be able to stop turning the pages of this warmhearted historical yuletide saga! 🩶

PS: Prepare to shed a few happy tears!

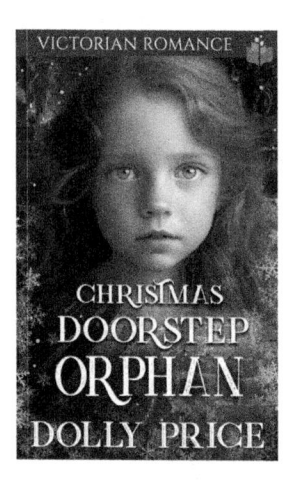

VICTORIAN ROMANCE

CHRISTMAS DOORSTEP ORPHAN

DOLLY PRICE

"Good morning, Colonel, and you, too, Madam. May I wish you both a very merry Christmas." The butler entered the breakfast room with a covered platter of hot sausages, bacon, eggs, smoked fish, and toast to serve the colonel and his lady personally, which he always did on special occasions.

"And we wish you the same, Perkins," replied his mistress. Her husband took the cover off the platter, and the delicious aroma of Christmas breakfast filled the room.

"There was a snowfall during the night," Mrs. Leigh-Donner said.

"It has begun again, Madam." Perkins looked toward the window, and their eyes followed his, just in time to see a carriage halt outside amid the whirling snowflakes.

"There is somebody out today," the colonel said. "It's too early to be Charlotte and the children. The neighbours have visitors, I expect."

The doorbell rang, startling them. Who could be at their door on Christmas morning?

"Excuse me," Perkins said, setting the platter down and making for the door.

"Very odd," remarked Colonel Leigh-Donner.

They heard voices in animated debate in the hallway.

Perkins burst into the room, rather quickly for his usual gravitas.

"It is a policeman, Colonel, to see you and Mrs. Leigh-Donner, and he bears a -" he stopped, for the constable was upon his heels and had entered the room. In his arms was a small child covered in a blanket, a woolly cap about the head. The child was asleep.

There was amazement.

"What, is he injured? Lay him on the easy chair, and we will fetch a doctor." Mrs. Leigh-Donner assumed that there had been an accident outside their door.

"No, it is not that." Perkins was red-faced and very agitated. "The constable says there is a note come with her."

Trembling, he thrust a piece of paper into the colonel's hands. There, he read, in bold capital letters, the following words.

MY NAME IS EMMA. I WAS BORN ON 1ST JULY 1859 IN A COUNTRY FAR AWAY. PLEASE TAKE ME TO MY PATERNAL GRANDPARENTS AT 11 ELIZABETH STREET, BELGRAVIA.

"Emma! My own name!" Mrs. Leigh-Donner fainted.

"She was found last night at Victoria Station in the ladies waiting room," said the constable. "She spent the night at the police station, wrapped up as warm as they could make 'er. Where shall I set the child?" He was getting impatient, for he wished to be rid of his burden, and he was forming the idea that the couple at this address had no wish to be acquainted with the child. It was a long way to a workhouse, and he had no wish to go there in a snowfall.

The housekeeper, Mrs. Breen, appeared then, and having been shown the note by Mr. Perkins, took the child from the constable, who made a hurried departure.

Assistance was found for her mistress, who was recovering. The colonel was stricken dumb.

"I shall take the child downstairs and give her milk," said Mrs. Breen. "What a shock!"

❄

Mrs. Leigh-Donner was able to sip some hot coffee and managed a slice of toast and a little poached egg. The colonel ate a hearty breakfast. He always said that eating helped him to think, and not even a shock like this would cause him to neglect his Christmas breakfast.

"Grandparents indeed! She cannot be our family," Emma said flatly. "Our boys are good boys."

The colonel said nothing. He had been in the army a long time and knew that plenty of young men sowed their wild oats while their mothers at home thought them saints.

They had two living sons, and neither was in England. Wesley was in India, a bachelor, he planned to marry when he returned on his next leave. He would hardly risk his chances with Lady Margaret Winston by sending home evidence of an indiscretion.

Lewis was in Italy on a European tour. They were in regular contact with Lewis; he was destined for Oxford and the Church. It could not be Lewis.

A silence ensued as there was one name left.

"Could it be...could it possibly be Cyril?" Emma asked in a very, very quiet voice.

The breakfast room was hung with doubt and possibility, hope and despair.

"No, it cannot be Cyril," her husband replied flatly and somewhat derisively.

"But, suppose he is alive?"

Cyril, the oldest son, was a captain in the British Army and had been missing, presumed dead, in the Crimea five years before.

"How could he be alive and not come home? How could he be alive and father a child in adultery? Have sense, Emma. Eat something."

"Charlotte will not like it," she admitted then, "if he is alive, and did not come home to her, and neglected her and the children all this time, and perhaps stayed in the Crimea and had a second family."

"It is a preposterous thought! Put it out of your head!"

"But he may be alive, just think! What if my Cyril is alive all this time! They never confirmed he was dead. They never found the bodies."

"He is dead, as are Corporals Brown and Enright."

Captain Cyril Leigh-Donner had led Corporals Richard Brown and James Enright up a steep hill on a scouting mission. An hour after they had left, the camp had heard shots from the hill. They had never been seen or heard of again in spite of extensive searches. They knew all three. Brown had been a young footman and Enright the coachman in the Leigh-Donner household. It had been a dreadful blow when they had heard the devastating news. The house had gone into a long mourning. The parents of the other two men lived in Spitalfields and Whitechapel, only a few miles from each other. Mrs. Leigh-Donner had visited them and given them consolation and help.

Mrs. Leigh-Donner rang the bell and ordered the child to be brought up to them. When she arrived, she was taken in her arms while she scrutinised her keenly.

"If you're looking for a resemblance, all infants look the same," her husband said, annoyed.

"She is getting past the infant stage, when resemblances begin to form. Do you not think that her eyes could look like ours, a little?"

"It's your imagination, Emma. Do not even begin to dream that Cyril is alive. This is not Cyril's child. He did not have fair hair."

She rumpled the thick fair tresses.

"Hair colour often changes!"

The child was awake and Emma, feeling restless, walked with her about the room. They came to a cabinet upon which was a group of photographs.

"Papa," sang the little one, pointing straight at a head and shoulders photo of Cyril.

"She is Cyril's! She is!" Mrs. Leigh-Donner became very excited. The colonel sighed in frustration and gulped back his coffee. If his son was alive and well somewhere, and in his wits, he was not only an adulterer, but a deserter and a disgrace. Better to believe him dead!

"It's Christmas morning, and Charlotte and the children will be here soon. Is all well with the kitchen preparations? Get your wits about you, Mrs. Leigh-Donner!" His black bushy eyebrows, the terror of his men, were drawn together in a frown.

"Yes, of course."

"Send the child down to the servants and we shall see what is to be done with her later on."

Mrs. Leigh-Donner pulled the bell again.

"Is my Cyril alive?" she asked herself, caressing her son's photograph. There must be some strange explanation for this, an explanation in which her son would come out blameless of course. He had lost his memory. That was it! He had married and regained his memory. But her ideas petered out in the improbability of it all.

❄

The housekeeper and butler said nothing downstairs about the note, and the staff were astounded at the sudden appearance of a child in their midst. She was placed in the care of the under housemaid while the servants prepared for their guests, Mrs. Cyril Leigh-Donner and her three children and their nursemaid.

They arrived at two o'clock full of Christmas merriment and gifts for their grandparents and sat down to a table laden with roast turkey stuffed with pork, baked ham dripping with syrup, golden roast potatoes, brussels sprouts, carrots, and lashings of gravy, with wine for the adults and lemonade for the children. But Charlotte noticed something wrong. Her parents-in-law were always a little sad about Cyril at Christmas, but always made the effort for the sake of the children. Today, even the jovial Grandfather was drawn and silent.

After sending the children out to play in the back garden after the Christmas pudding had been served, she asked them what the matter was. They had no choice but to inform her of the morning's happenings and to show her the note.

"It can't be Cyril," she said, her voice tremulous.

"Why not?" her mother-in-law asked sharply.

"He is dead."

"Quite so, Charlotte," Colonel Leigh-Donner said.

Charlotte's hands were shaking; she put her coffee cup back on the saucer with a giveaway tinkle. She had fallen out of love with Cyril a few years after they married, and he with her. They had been very young, she seventeen, he twenty. He had not been a bad man, but authoritarian like his father, and she had begun to suffer under his tight control and domineering way. While she never wished him dead, after seven years she would be free to remarry if he did not return. She was in love again, and Mr.

Marshall was patiently waiting until she could be declared free.

"It cannot be Cyril," she said flatly.

"She pointed to his portrait and said 'Papa,'" Mrs. Leigh-Donner said firmly. There was a very uncomfortable silence.

"What will you do with her?" Charlotte asked.

"We do not know," her father-in-law said.

"It must be a hoax," Charlotte went on. "It is well known you have a son missing, presumed dead, and someone wants a good place for their illegitimate, nobody child. Is there no way to find out for certain?"

"It appears there is not," Mrs. Leigh-Donner said. "Her clothes are not of the best quality but decent, and she is clean. She has been taken care of. She has a few words, but they are unintelligible."

After dinner, Charlotte went downstairs to the servant's hall to see the child for herself. She was sleeping on a small couch, two chairs drawn up close to it to prevent her from falling off. She gazed at her and satisfied herself that she looked nothing like Cyril's other children.

"She looks common," was her verdict. "It's a hoax, a deception, to get her a good life. She has a cunning parent who would risk that, but it is so cruel to pretend that Cyril is alive, when he is not! And why do my in-laws not think of their other two sons? It would be a good trick indeed, for either of them, to point a finger at Cyril's being alive, when they know he is not."

When her mother-in-law asked her to take the baby home with her because she had a nursery, she refused, and left that evening in a very bad temper. Unlike the first Christmas, this Christmas had been ruined by the arrival of a small child...

❄

What will happen to this unwanted babe? How will the bairn's future unfold? Continue reading this unforgettable story in Christmas Doorstep Orphan, the new Christmas novel by Dolly Price.

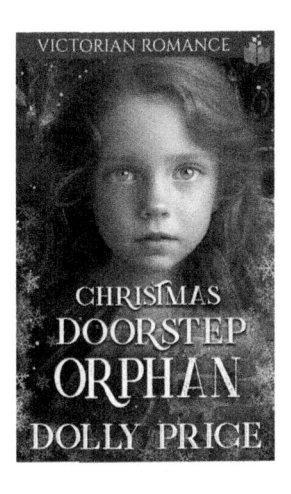

Continue Reading Christmas Doorstep Orphan on Amazon

OUR GIFT TO YOU

AS A WAY TO SAY THANK YOU WE WOULD LOVE TO SEND YOU THIS BEAUTIFUL STORY FREE OF CHARGE.

Click here for your free copy of Whitechapel Waif

PureRead.com/victorian

At PureRead we publish books you can trust. Great tales without smut or swearing, but with all of the mystery and romance you expect from a great story.

Be the first to know when we release new books, take part in our fun competitions, and get surprise free books in your inbox by signing up to our free VIP Reader list.

As a welcome gift you'll receive the story of the Whitechapel Waif straight to your inbox...

Click here for your free copy of Whitechapel Waif

PureRead.com/victorian

Printed in Great Britain
by Amazon